"Family is everything to me," Alice said. "Can't you understand?"

"Oh, I know all about family," Jonah replied. He looked straight into her eyes. "My biological mother was a Mayeaux and I managed to trace her back to Bayou Rosette. I'm pretty sure she was one of the younger sisters of the infamous Mayeux brothers."

Alice had to grab the nearest chair for support. "Wow."

"Yeah, wow. When I read the article you wrote about this bayou, it triggered something in me, Alice. So yes, I did come here to build houses, to rebuild, but while I'm here, I'd like to find out something about my roots. My lack of roots. Why did my mother give me up? That's the big question."

Alice's heart turned to mush. She could see the torment in his eyes. "I'd be willing to help you answer that question…if you want."

Books by Lenora Worth

Love Inspired

The Wedding Quilt
Logan's Child
I'll Be Home for Christmas
Wedding at Wildwood
His Brother's Wife
Ben's Bundle of Joy
The Reluctant Hero
One Golden Christmas
†*When Love Came to Town*
†*Something Beautiful*
†*Lacey's Retreat*
Easter Blessings
"The Lily Field"
‡*The Carpenter's Wife*
‡*Heart of Stone*
‡*A Tender Touch*
Blessed Bouquets
"The Dream Man"
**A Certain Hope*
**A Perfect Love*
**A Leap of Faith*
Christmas Homecoming
Mountain Sanctuary
Lone Star Secret
Gift of Wonder

†In the Garden
‡Sunset Island
*Texas Hearts

Love Inspired Suspense

Fatal Image
Secret Agent Minister
Deadly Texas Rose
A Face in the Shadows
Heart of the Night
Code of Honor

LENORA WORTH

has written more than thirty books, most of those for Steeple Hill. She also works freelance for a local magazine, where she has written monthly opinion columns, feature articles and social commentaries. She also wrote for five years for the local paper. Married to her high-school sweetheart for thirty-three years, Lenora lives in Louisiana and has two grown children and a cat. She loves to read, take long walks and sit in her garden.

Gift of Wonder

Lenora Worth

Steeple
Hill®

Published by Steeple Hill Books™

STEEPLE HILL BOOKS

ISBN-13: 978-0-373-81421-3

GIFT OF WONDER

This edition published by arrangement with Steeple Hill Books.

www.SteepleHill.com

Printed in U.S.A.

He performs wonders that cannot be fathomed,
miracles that cannot be counted

—*Job* 5:9

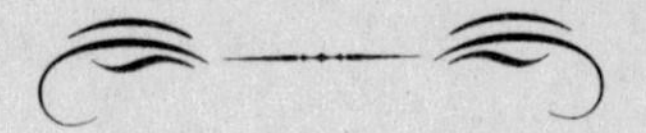

To Community Renewal International.
Because I CARE!

Chapter One

"Who in the world is that?"

Alice Bryson put down her iced tea and stood against the balustrade of the old front porch so she could stare across Bayou Rosette at the man walking underneath the oaks along the opposite shore.

Her older sister, Lorene Hobert, glanced up from her cross-stitching, squinting in the late-afternoon sun to get a better glimpse of the stranger about forty yards away on the other side of the marshy bank. "Well, he's certainly a tall drink of water, isn't he?"

"I'll say," Alice replied, her hand going up to shade her eyes as she watched the attractive brown-haired man meticulously measuring off the property with his booted feet. "He has some sort of gadget in his hand.

Looks like a pocket watch or a cell phone. He seems to be talking to it."

"Maybe it's a compass," Lorene said, chuckling. "Maybe he's lost and disoriented. Of course, I talk to myself a lot, too."

Alice grinned at that. "If he's a city boy, he just might be lost." And the way he was dressed in a lightweight gray suit and crisp blue shirt indicated he sure wasn't from around these parts.

"Why don't you walk across the footbridge and help the poor fellow," Lorene suggested, her ever-present matchmaking skills shining through. As the older, married Bryson sister, Lorene, who was expecting her first child in a few weeks, deemed it necessary to introduce Alice to every available man in sight. Even perfect strangers.

"Why would he be measuring off land with his feet if he's lost?" Alice asked while she admired the man's muscular, athletic frame and his shiny, light brown hair.

Lorene stopped stitching again, then lowered her needlepoint frame onto her growing belly. "He might be a surveyor. Remember all those rumors in town that some big company's coming in to build a whole new community—to replace the houses lost from the hurricane? Maybe he's scouting for land or something."

Alice shot a look at her sister to see if she was being sarcastic. Lorene glowed with good health. Pregnancy sure agreed with her. Lorene's blue eyes sparkled and her freckled, fair skin shimmered, partly from that glow and partly from the late-fall heat of southern Louisiana. But Lorene looked pretty…and in love. But not sarcastic. Good, Alice thought with relief. She didn't need any teasing remarks today.

She huffed a breath and hid the tinge of envy she felt toward her sister. Then she quickly replaced the envy with thankful thoughts as she asked God to continue blessing Lorene. And her. While their old homeplace had survived the hurricane, not everyone had been so lucky. Most of the homes around here had suffered some sort of damage. And many across the bayou, where the wind and water had been worse, had been torn down.

"I've heard those same rumors, of course," she said as she sank back against one of the wide porch-posts. "But they were never substantiated, so I couldn't write anything based on rumors. Even tried to get the mayor to talk to me about this. But I never believed anything would actually happen, in spite of the buzz. We've been forgotten here on Bayou Rosette."

"Not entirely," Lorene replied, taking up her work again. "Jay says the word in church this morning was that some big corporation *is* going to rebuild the whole town but with a more environmentally sound and economical plan—seems Bayou Rosette is going green."

"Are you sure? I think I would have heard something down at the magazine if anything definite had been decided."

"It's hush-hush, according to Jay." Lorene stretched, then rubbed her stomach. "But he heard it straight from a town council member. Strictly confidential, so don't go telling anyone at the magazine about this."

Alice let out a groan. "You know I can't do that without stirring the pot. So why didn't you say something sooner, anyway?"

Lorene looked apologetic. "I forgot about it after we got home from church. I had one thing on my mind—eating lunch. And I'm getting hungry again. I'll heat up the pot roast when Jay gets back from his meeting."

Alice turned back toward the man across

the way. "You might be right about our mysterious visitor. It has been quiet around here lately. Too quiet. Nobody's talking at all, but I've got a feeling that a lot of behind-the-scenes action *has* been brewing. But we have to be careful about this."

Lorene's look went from apologetic to sympathetic. "You can't judge every stranger by one bad example, Alice."

"I'm not judging anyone," Alice retorted, hating the pity in her sister's eyes. "I'm withholding judgment. But I want proof this time." Which was probably why she hadn't pushed the officials around here to verify the rumors. Maybe she didn't want to know or be involved after what had happened with the last pipe dream around here.

Lorene shrugged. "I'm telling you, things could be about to change, and for the better. We're going green."

Wondering how her sister always heard the interesting gossip before she did—since *she* was the reporter—Alice said, "Sister, we can't get much greener." She swept a hand across the view of slow-moving black water and bald cypress trees covered with Spanish moss, then inhaled deeply. "Smell that?" The scent of nature's decay mixed with the tart smell of the last of the bright red summer geraniums lining the long porch. "This place is the very essence of green."

"I'm talking about green houses—it's the new thing, don't you know? And when you think about it, the Bible does tell us to harm neither the earth nor the seas. It's all about conserving energy, making the most of the sun and the water. Making sure houses are a bit safer next time a big one comes through."

Alice knew what a "big one" meant. They lived on a bayou that fed into the Mississippi River fifty miles north of New Orleans. The risk of another major storm brewing in the Gulf, even this late in the year, was never far from their minds. Fall in Louisiana was prime hurricane season.

"You really think that's why he's over there muttering to himself?" She twisted to stare at the man across the way. He had yet to look up. "Do you think he's a contractor?"

"I sure hope not," Lorene said. "You did run that last one out of town on a rail."

"That's because he was a cheater and a crook," Alice replied. And he'd sure had her fooled, right up till their wedding day. He was also a liar who'd left her at the altar after she'd questioned his motives. "I won't tolerate any more con artists sniffing around here." She directed her gaze back across the water. "I can't take that again."

"Go find out who he is," Lorene said, shaking her head. "Or better yet, do an article on him for the *Bayou Buzz*. I'm sure Dotty would approve."

"Not if I don't have my facts straight, she won't. She's still a tad bitter about my canceled wedding, too."

"Well, then, this time just make sure you get all the facts right up front," Lorene replied. "We all get fooled sometimes, you know."

"And like I said, I don't intend to let it happen again," Alice replied.

"Then go over there and ask the man what he's doing."

Alice stood straight up, then pushed a hand through her curly, sandy-blond bob. Her savvy editor and publisher, Dotty Tillman, would love to get a scoop on any kind of new industry coming to town. And since Alice was senior reporter for the monthly magazine—well, she was the *only* reporter for the small-budget local publication—she'd certainly want to write the article. But she had to be sure. And what better way to be certain than to get the news straight from the horse's mouth? But this time she'd handle things much differently. This time she'd stay professional and aloof. And she'd make sure this one was honest.

Deciding that, she turned to her sister. "That's not a bad idea—me going over there to have a talk with him. I've been trying to find something interesting for next month's cover story. At least I can find out why he's here. You know, just to separate fact from fiction. Off the record, since it's Sunday."

"That is your job," Lorene countered, grinning prettily. "Even if it is Sunday. And I'll finish up here and head in to get supper going before Jay comes home."

"That is your job," Alice shot over her shoulder with a mimic as she headed down the steps and out into the tree-shaded yard. "Even if it is Sunday."

Her sister's laughter echoed after her. They both kept the tradition of quiet Sundays at home by going to church then taking this one afternoon to spend time with each other. That had been important when their parents were alive. And it still was, now that their parents were buried in the old cemetery at the Rosette Church down the road and they were both grown up and living separate lives in this big, old, rambling Creole-style house.

Separate, but together, with each sister having her own space now that Lorene was married. Since there were plenty of rooms to choose from in the twelve-room house, Alice had taken one end of the upstairs and redone it into an efficiency apartment, using the old outside stairs as a private entrance. Lorene and Jay had redone the bottom floor and the rest of the upstairs across the wide hallway. It worked for both sisters, and Jay didn't mind as long as he had Lorene to come home to every night.

A perfect setup.

Even if she's married and happy and I'm still single and…searching, Alice thought, memories of her almost-wedding hitting her as she glanced out across the dark bayou water.

And that's when the stranger across the way finally looked up and right into Alice's eyes.

Jonah had read and reread the story about the old plantation house across the bayou. Had heard the amazing tale of how the stubborn Bryson sisters had refused to leave the house when a major storm had hit a couple of years ago. The water had risen to the upstairs front porch and stopped, or so the story went. Two of the ancient live oaks had toppled over. But not onto the beautiful two-hundred-year-old house. No, the big oaks had fallen away from the house. The bottom floor ruined, a few shingles ripped away, some leakage in the old upstairs kitchen, bramble and branches everywhere and a couple of snakes and baby alligators on the loose, but…Rosette House had survived and the Bryson legend had endured.

He knew the story of Rosette House—constructed on a sugarcane plantation in the early eighteen hundreds, almost destroyed by the Civil War, but rebuilt by a family member who came back to Louisiana to mend his war wounds and to start again. That created a turn-of-the-century success story about the feisty female ancestor of the two women who lived here now. Rosette Benoit Bryson had arrived a bride from New Orleans, come to live on the once-nameless bayou her new groom had formally named after her, in the rebuilt house he'd also named after her. The man sure had been smitten.

And while Rosette Bryson's story had captivated Jonah since he'd first recognized the familiar house in the picture in the paper, he wasn't sure what to expect as he watched the pretty blonde in the jeans and old Tulane sweatshirt sauntering across the weathered wooden footbridge. He was pretty sure this was the woman who'd written that historic account in the local *Bayou Buzz* magazine—an account that had been picked up by the *Times-Picayune,* where he'd read it with a growing interest a few months ago. But he wasn't about to tell her that he'd seen the house long before he'd ever read her account of it. His heart boomed against his ribs as he watched her. Her story had started him on this impulsive quest to find out about his own past while he tried to build a whole new community. Did he dare ask her if she knew the Mayeaux?

No, not yet. He had plenty of time to research his family tree. To waylay the dread in that, he thought back over the story he'd read. Poor Sam Bryson had only lived five years after he'd brought his bride here. Rosette had gone on to farm the land, build a church in memory of her late husband, start a town in order to run her sugarcane mill and raise his sons to be fine, upstanding citizens—and she'd lived to be ninety-six. Very impressive.

As was the woman walking toward him now with a hesitant smile on her heart-shaped face. Obviously one of the famous Bryson girls.

The single one, from what he'd heard in town.

"Hey there," Alice said, suddenly shy. He was even better looking up close. His gray eyes reminded her of the Spanish moss at night, full of mystery, shimmering with possibility.

"Hi," he said, stepping forward to greet her. "I guess you're wondering what I'm doing."

"Thought did cross my mind." She shrugged, pushed at her worn college sweatshirt. "I mean, we don't often get people all suited up and running around the swamp talking to themselves. Who are you?"

"Direct. I like that." He extended his hand. "I'm Jonah Sheridan."

She took his hand. "Like Jonah and the whale?"

He actually chuckled, but he shook her hand and then released it, leaving a warm impression. "Something like that, yes. Or at least I'm feeling that way right now."

She liked that he seemed nervous. It gave her the upper hand. "Relax. We don't see many whales on the bayou."

"That's good. I stay in enough trouble as it is."

She pushed at her curly hair. "And why is that?"

He held up the electronic gadget in his hand. "Oh, people think I'm strange. I take copious notes. I wasn't exactly talking to myself. This is a tape recorder. Helps me to stay *out* of trouble."

"I use a tape recorder myself sometimes," she replied. "I'm a reporter for the *Bayou Buzz* magazine."

His eyes widened. "So it is you. You're—"

Surprised, she nodded. "Alice Bryson. The one and only. And how do you know me?"

He grinned and lowered his head. "I saw your article about the history of Rosette House a few months ago—it was reprinted in the New Orleans newspaper. I actually have a copy back in my room at the bed-and-breakfast in town." He pointed to the house. "Since I'm a history buff, I decided to read up on this area. I was interested in how you rebuilt the bottom floor of the house after the storm."

Alice scrutinized him for sincerity but couldn't tell for sure. Did she sense hesitancy in him? Or was he holding back something important, maybe trying to pull the wool over her eyes? "Well, that's good to know. My editor wasn't sure we should run with that cover story, but I convinced her."

"I just reckon you did."

"I was pleasantly surprised when the newspaper picked it up. It's been good for business around here."

"It sure got *me* interested."

"Oh, yeah—and just what *are* you doing in our small town?"

"You don't mince words, do you?"

She grinned. "Some say I'm way too blunt. I just believe in cutting to the chase."

He put the tape recorder in his pocket, then put his hands on his hips. "Well, it's supposed to be a secret right now."

Alice hid the excitement making her pulse race. She was way too nosy for her own good, but that also made her job a lot more interesting and challenging. "Off the record?"

"If you don't mind, yes. It's been in the works for months now and soon everyone will know, but I'm here to plan a new community and I just got here this morning to officially get things started. Permits, contracts and all that."

"Yeah, and all that. We'd heard rumors but no one around here would talk. The mayor's been tight-lipped. The chamber of commerce wouldn't budge, so we just had to sit and wait. I don't like sitting and waiting."

He nodded, then blew out a breath, his earnest gaze clashing with her doubting one. "Can you sit on this a bit longer, just until I get everything lined up for the town meeting next week?"

Alice didn't like that request. "Maybe, if you level with me."

"I *am* leveling with you." He raised a hand. "Look around. This land is a mess. I'd like to rebuild it, only better."

"You mean, all bright and new and green, right?"

"Word does spread around here."

"Yep. And we're all for improving things, but… you'll have to do a lot of tall talking to make this stick."

"I plan to," he said. "That's why I'm out here talking to myself. I've had people out here, checking around, but I wanted to see the land with my own eyes."

Alice didn't know why he made her fidget, maybe because right this very minute he wasn't looking at the land. He was looking at her. She wasn't shy; she loved to talk it up with people and she was a born extrovert. That's how she got the best angles for her feature stories. But this interesting stranger made her want to fluff her hair and put on lipstick. To ward off these strange feelings, she said, "You know, Einstein said, 'Why remember it when you can write it down.' I guess it's the same with recording it, huh?"

"Exactly." He twirled a finger by his ear. "Sometimes, I get so much going inside my head I go into overload. I have all these plans—"

"For our little bayou."

"Yes." He pointed to the south. "You know it's worse down that way. I want to build nice, comfortable, affordable houses so that everyone who had to leave this area can come home again. And I think the local economy would be better for it, too."

Alice stared at him, wondering why he was so enthusiastic about a town he'd just discovered a few months ago. "What brought you here to Bayou Rosette, anyway? I can't see you coming here just because of my article, so why us?"

He glanced over at her house then back into her eyes. "Honestly, it *was* your magazine article, Alice. I read the story of Rosette Benoit Bryson and what you wrote about the house, but you also wrote about the history of your family…and about how dire things were after the hurricane hit. You said you wanted people to know about your bayou and your town, you wanted them to remember the past so they could rebuild for the future. That's kinda the way I think, too. After I read it, I did my research and I knew I had to come down here and meet Rosette's descendants. Especially the one who'd written with such pride about her ancestors. Your article made me want to do something to help this community."

Alice didn't know how to respond to that. So she just said, "Thank you. But it has to be more than that."

He leaned forward, his expression solemn and sure. "It's a whole lot more, yes. But for now, I can honestly say *you're* the main reason I'm here."

Chapter Two

"I beg your pardon? What do you mean, I'm the *main* reason you're here?" She stepped closer. "You said there was a lot more to it and I think I need to know what that means."

Jonah slapped at a mosquito buzzing by his ear. He shouldn't have blurted that out, but it was the truth. Well, part of the truth, at least. But since she looked as if she might bolt away like a frightened doe, he tried to explain. "Your article, I mean. I told you I'm a history buff and reading your article made me want to see more of Bayou Rosette. And because of that, I decided to invest in this place."

She looked doubtful. "So, let me get this straight. You read my article and *that* caused you to want to build houses across from Rosette House?"

"Yes." He wasn't one for sweating under pressure, but the way her big blue eyes filled with distrust made him think he was on a witness stand. What would she say if he told her the complete truth of why he was here—that he was pretty sure his relatives had once lived across the bayou from her, right here where they were standing. Since he couldn't begin to tell her something he wasn't even sure of himself, he only said, "Your words inspired me."

That much was true. But more importantly, her thorough history had convinced Jonah he'd finally found a link to his past.

She burst out laughing. "Now, that's a new one."

"What do you mean?"

She wiped at her eyes and grinned at him. "Do you honestly expect me to believe my little feature article on the history of this house and this backwater bayou inspired you to want to come here and build houses and do good for our little town?"

"Well, yes, but when you put it like that—"

"Where exactly did you come from, anyway?"

"Shreveport," he said, hitting at the buzz in his ear again. "These mosquitoes are getting worse now that dusk is coming."

"Bring bug spray next time," she suggested, her hands on her hips. "What do you do in Shreveport—besides being a history buff?"

"I'm a builder and an architect. I own a land development company—JS Building and Development, Inc. I buy up property and redevelop it."

Her eyes narrowed, then brightened with a dangerous glint. "Well, at least you have the right credentials."

"Yes, I do. I've built office complexes and parks. I helped remodel a whole building in downtown Shreveport a couple of years ago. It's a complete model for green living."

"*Green living* sure is the buzzword with you. Even more buzzy than these pesky mosquitoes."

"It's a good way to rebuild, don't you think?"

"I'm still trying to decide, but it sounds reasonable."

Thinking he was making some headway, he hit at a mosquito on his jacket sleeve and sent the poor creature to its demise. He wasn't ready to explain how seeing this particular house on a newspaper page had caused him to drop everything and head south. That was personal. Too personal. Especially when she was glaring at him with what looked like deadly intent.

He tried again. "I want to help this community. And I've done studies, I've researched this area's economy and I've talked to several local businessmen and officials. They've all grilled me about budgets and permits and codes and economic impact, but you're the first person to question my *motives.*"

She pushed at her unruly golden hair. "Maybe that's because I'm the person living right across the water. Maybe because I like things the way they are—nice and quiet and private."

"But…you had neighbors before." He pointed to the remains of a small cottage around the curve in the bayou. He knew she'd had neighbors. He'd fully researched her former neighbors while trying to find his relatives. "Don't you want neighbors again?"

She looked at him then glanced around. "I don't know. Where we're standing has always been kind of empty and overgrown, but I got used to it that way. I think someone lived over here long ago, but that family moved away before I was even born."

"Did your families get along?"

She put her hands on her hips, probably wondering what kind of question that was for a developer to be asking. "Not always, but we managed. Some of our past neighbors haven't been exactly friendly, according to my older sister. It's kinda pleasant out here now. Or it was until today."

"You can't be serious?"

She shook her head and finally smiled. "I'm just messing with you on that account. Yes, I miss all of the old neighbors—the ones I remember from around the bend here. A lot. But…I'm not so sure I want a whole new community right across from my house. And I'm really not sure about you and why you want to build here. Can't you find work up in Shreveport?"

"Yes, I have plenty of work. And my employees are working around the clock on several different projects, including this one. We're solid."

"Uh-huh. So solid you dropped everything to rush down here and measure land right across from my home."

"It wouldn't be directly across from you," he said. "I see this as a good investment, an economic prospect that will create jobs and housing. But it shouldn't interfere with your property at all—I was actually measuring right here for a park, maybe. A small park with a swing and benches and a walking trail leading to the homes. But I do plan on buying up the land next to yours. The actual community would be around the curve in the bayou."

"But what about this land we're standing on? How are you gonna buy it and build a park on it? Like I said, the people who lived here moved away a long time ago. And since then, this land has turned into part of the swamp."

Jonah gave her the barest of answers. "They sold it to someone else when they left. I had one of my brokers track down that owner and we made him an offer. He seemed glad to be rid of it."

"Yes, I imagine he is at that. I never knew who bought it from the Mayeaux. Whoever it was didn't bother to mow it or keep it clean. Somebody did finally come and take away what was left of the old house after the hurricane."

Jonah tried not to flinch. She'd just verified what he needed to know. The Mayeaux family had lived right here on this land at one time. But he'd bought it from someone else. And now it was his. Kind of ironic and all the more proof that he was meant to be here. "I'll keep it clean, I can promise you that. It's gonna look a lot better once we get this subdivision up."

"That's good. It tends to draw snakes and other creepy things." She turned to leave. "Now go on back to the Bayou Belle Inn and put some calamine lotion on those bug bites."

Jonah's relief was instant but he hid it behind trying to win her over. He would have thought she'd be the first one in line behind him on this project. "Hey, wait. Don't you want to hear more?"

"I think I've heard enough. You're going to come in and rebuild this community. That's good for everyone, I'd think."

She wasn't as excited as he'd hoped. "I'll be right here for the duration, if you have any questions. And I'll keep tabs on things long after we're finished, of course. This project means—"

She whirled then, her eyes bright with misgivings. "What does it mean—for you? I know what it will mean to the people of this town and I truly hope you succeed, because we need a little hope around here."

Seeing her doubt and a bit of sadness in her eyes, Jonah followed her across the arched bridge. "But you don't believe I can do it, do you?"

She stopped, turned to face him. Her eyes had lost some of their fire. Now she looked gloomy, her whole body going still and quiet. "After the hurricane, things were bad around here. We were mostly cut off from the rest of the world. But we weren't cut off from the scams. Some of our neighbors got taken advantage of, big-time." She looked out over the old oak trees lining her side of the bank. "A lot of us got our feelings hurt. We trusted too quickly, because we were still reeling from all that had happened. So excuse me if I don't exactly believe in a pretty boy with big promises of a grand scheme."

He let that settle for a few seconds, then said, "First, I don't do scams. I'm a legitimate businessman and I'm good at what I do—and your entire town council has checked and rechecked my credentials. Second, I'd never take advantage of anyone. I believe in solid investments, but I also believe in being efficient, economical and energy conscious. And third, do you really think I'm a 'pretty boy'?"

She gave him a look that would have made an alligator grit his teeth and go back underwater. "I've seen your kind before, hotshot. And yes, I'm learning to question everything and everybody these days. So while I wish you the best, I'm not convinced." With that she took off walking across the rickety old bridge, her arms swinging, her hair bouncing. "Nice talking to you. See you at the next town hall meeting. I'll be there with my tape recorder."

Jonah swallowed, took a breath then called, "Hey, you never did answer my question. Do you think I'm—"

She held up a hand but kept walking. "You don't want to know what I think about you right now, trust me."

Trust *her?* He wanted to laugh out loud. But he didn't dare. Before he could trust her, he'd probably have to work double time just to get *her* to trust *him.* He couldn't have her writing a scathing article about his plans. That wouldn't work at all. Because she might dig too deep and find out the whole story behind his sudden, impulsive need to build on this ground. The Bryson sisters obviously carried a lot of weight in this town. He'd need their support, or his hopes and dreams could sink in the water.

But how was he supposed to win her over

when he couldn't even begin to explain why he'd taken a leave of absence from his own firm to come down here to personally supervise this project? How did a man explain to a complete stranger that he needed to know about this land and this town because he might have roots here?

He stared at her until she reached the steps leading to the second-story porch of the big, square white house, then shouted, "Can't we sit down and discuss this a little more?"

"See you at the meeting," she replied. Then she turned and waved to him before disappearing with a flounce through the screen door.

It swung wide and banged out a warning as it fell back against the door frame. A loud warning.

"Are you coming down for dinner?"

Alice heard the hidden question in her sister's demand: Are you coming down to tell me everything and I mean everything because I watched the whole thing through the window and I'm dying to know.

She wasn't in the mood to talk. But she was in the mood for biscuits and leftover pot roast. "I'll be there in a couple of minutes."

Going to the tall windows of her cozy kitchen-and-den combination on the top left side of the house, she checked to make sure *he* was gone. When she didn't see him in the growing dusk, she passed a hand over her hair then headed down the steps from her private apartment to the front door of the house.

The stairs leading down from the second floor made it easy for Alice to scoot down for meals with her sister and brother-in-law. But she tried to give them their privacy, so she didn't make this a habit.

Except for Sundays. Sundays would always be family day at Rosette House. And tonight, as the sun sank in a swirl of pink and gold across the bayou and the frogs and cicadas started singing out in the swamp, she needed to be with family. Why was dusk always such a lonely time of day?

Putting thoughts of Jonah Sheridan out of her mind, Alice admired the bright orange pumpkins and lush yellow-and-red mums Lorene had arranged on a fresh bale of hay by the door. Her sister and Jay had remodeled what used to be considered the basement into a beautiful country kitchen and a huge hearth room, complete with the original fireplace and chimney. There was a breakfast nook in the kitchen and a formal dining room and tiny powder room across the wide hall on the other side of the house. Today, the tall French doors were thrown open to the late-autumn breezes flowing through the cross-ventilated rooms.

When Alice came through the double French doors into the breakfast room, the smell of fresh biscuits and pot roast wafted out to greet her and made her think of her parents. She could almost hear her mother's gentle laughter, could see her daddy's twinkling blue eyes. How she missed them.

But she had Lorene and Jay and soon they'd all have a baby to spoil. "Want me to pour the tea?" she said by way of a greeting.

"Sure," Lorene said, glancing up as if to gauge Alice's mood. "Have you been working?"

"No. Just folding some clothes and checking e-mail, nothing special."

Jay looked from his wife to Alice, his dark brown eyes questioning. He knew they had their own kind of language, or at least he accused them of that very thing. A language full of feminine undertones and hushed whispers, he'd say. Alice pitied the poor man. He always squinted whenever they got going with the small talk that meant big talk later.

Jay wanted to understand but he never would, really. Her brother-in-law was more comfortable out on a tractor, farming the land, than he was trying to figure out women. So now, in typical, quiet Jay fashion, he just sat and listened until they'd talked all around the subject not yet mentioned.

Then he said, "Let's say grace and get to that pot roast."

Lorene giggled like a schoolgirl. Alice smiled and grabbed their hands. And stewed about Jonah Sheridan while Jay said a lovely blessing. When she opened her eyes, her shrewd sister was staring at her. "Okay, start talking, Alice. What did you find out from our mysterious visitor?"

Jonah was stewing away over a cup of coffee in the tiny diner on the bottom floor of the Bayou Belle Inn. He was beginning to doubt his own sanity. Why had he come here? Oh, yeah. He wanted to build a new community on Bayou Rosette and he wanted to find out about the family who'd lived across from Rosette House. Two lofty notions, but he was willing to work on both—one to keep him busy and the other to finally find some closure in his life. If a certain curly-haired blonde with a hefty attitude didn't get in his way. Or discover the truth before he ever broke ground.

"Why you look so glum, *mon ami?*"

Jonah looked up to find the proprietor of the Belle staring at him with a hangdog expression. Jimmy Germain had a gray beard and a little bit of gray hair to match on the back of his round head. He was short and husky and laughed with a robust belly bounce. His wife, Paulette, was also short and wide and very friendly. They made a good team and they cooked some good food.

So why wasn't Jonah eating his crawfish po'boy?

"I went out to look at Rosette House today," he explained. He had to be very careful what he said since the rumors were already flying fast and furious.

"Did the girls give you a tour of the old place?"

Jonah's moroseness lifted at that question. "They give tours?"

"If you ask real nice, sure."

"Oh, well, then I guess I won't be invited in for a tour. I met *one* of the Bryson sisters today."

Jimmy's grin widened and the belly

bounce began as he chuckled so hard his ruddy complexion beamed scarlet. "I'm guessing it wasn't sweet Lorene."

"No…it was the other sister. Alice."

"Oo-wee! She's a firecracker, for sure."

"You can say that again," Jonah replied, grabbing a crispy fried crawfish tail off his sandwich. He popped the spicy tidbit in his mouth and chewed. "What's her story, anyway? I mean, I know she's single and she works at the *Bayou Buzz* and all that. But…is there something else I need to know?"

Jimmy leaned close. "That, my friend, would require about three hours of my valuable time."

Jonah ate another crawfish. "I got nowhere to go. Talk to me."

Jimmy's eyes shifted as he put his beefy elbows on the mahogany counter. "Alice, she has trust issues with men."

"You don't say."

Jimmy nodded. "Right after the storm when things were so bad around here, she fell for a contractor who was passing through. He took on work—remodeling and such—and he also took off with some of our hard-earned money in the process. Never finished the work." He shook his head. "And the worst of it—Alice believed in him, thought he'd come to help us. But he was just a greedy man who'd come to take advantage of us. He took advantage of Alice's good graces, too. He had her up to the altar, ready to marry him, probably just so he could get his hands on her inheritance. But she got wind of his shenanigans and questioned him minutes before the wedding. He denied all of it, then he blamed her for not believing in him. He left, just like that. On to the next town, I reckon. Left that pretty little bride heartbroken and humiliated. She's not over that yet. Might not ever be over it."

Jonah pushed the rest of his sandwich away. Alice had said as much. She'd said they'd all been taken advantage of. That some of them had been hurt.

And she was the one who'd been hurt the most, from the way she'd acted today. And no wonder. A jilted bride. Jilted by a man who'd offered her hope while he swindled everyone in town. Just as Jonah had offered her hope today with all his big plans.

"It's worse than I thought," he said, staring into his cold coffee. "She must think I'm like that. But I'm not. Not at all. I could never leave my bride at the altar." Especially if she sparkled with life the way Alice did, part fire and part flowers.

Jimmy patted his meaty hand on the counter, his words full of sympathy. "Yep. A woman scorned. It ain't good, that's for sure."

Jonah paid Jimmy and bid him good-night. Then he walked out and stared down the long main street of Bayou Rosette. And he wondered what was going through Alice Bryson's mind right now.

Was she thinking about him? Or was she thinking up ways to stop him before he ever got started, just to prove a point about some idiot who'd done her wrong? And why did he care, anyway? He'd get the job done. He'd build his community. He wanted to do this. Had to do it, for more reasons than he could explain or even justify to himself. But he'd never factored in that the woman who'd inadvertently caused him to come down here on this crazy whim might also turn out to be the very one who'd put a crimp in his plans. Maybe he should just go back to Shreveport.

You're not a quitter, he told himself. You've dealt with much worse than a jilted blonde with an ax to grind. And he'd always done things on his own terms, even though Aunt Nancy had urged him to turn to God for guidance.

But Jonah didn't need God's help on this. He just needed Alice Bryson to play nice and let him do his job. And he hoped while he was here he could find the truth at last. He wasn't concerned so much about Alice. He'd get around her and build his new community, one way or another. But he was concerned about those questions he'd had all his life. What if he didn't like the answers?

Maybe that was why he was so worried he hadn't been able to finish eating the best crawfish po'boy he'd ever tasted.

Alice Bryson was just one person. One very forceful person. He'd worked for months on clearing the way for approval so he could get the whole town in on this renovation. He'd make them believe he could do this. He had to. Because he needed to do this. He'd come on this quest, this journey, to fulfill his creative need to build things, but the main reason he was here was to fill that empty place deep inside his soul.

He didn't exactly want to call it a "God moment," as some of his friends back home might say, but it sure had seemed that way when he'd stumbled across Alice's intriguing story. He had to help Bayou Rosette. Because he was pretty sure he came from the

Mayeaux family and that this was the place where his biological mother had been born and raised, right across the bayou from Rosette House.

And somehow, while he was here he had to find out why that same mother had abandoned him and never looked back.

Chapter Three

"I don't understand why you were so rude to the man."

Shoving her floral tote bag and her purse into her yellow vintage Volkswagen, Alice closed her eyes and counted to ten to drown out her sister's voice. How could she explain to Lorene that Jonah Sheridan reminded her of all she'd lost? She'd placed her heart in a stranger's hand once before and look where that had gotten her. Jilted and tossed aside, left embarrassed and bitter.

"Alice, are you listening to me?"

Alice turned at the door of her car. "I hear you loud and clear, Lorene, and I've tried to tell you how I feel. The man has this lofty plan. It just sounds too good to be true to me. And I wasn't rude. I just didn't get all giddy when he went on and on about building a new community across from us."

"Not right across," Lorene reminded her. "I think a park would be wonderful across the bridge. "I could take the baby for walks over there."

Alice shook her head. "I knew better than to tell you anything. You can't go spreading that around. Everything he told me was off the record."

"I understand," Lorene said, holding the water hose out to send a spray over her geraniums and mums. "I won't say a word. But I'm sure the whole town is speculating about what he wants to do, since I've had phone calls all day about it."

"And that's just it," Alice replied, getting in the tiny convertible. "It's all speculation and I'm tired of speculators and curiosity seekers and people thinking they can just come in and take over and make things better again. They can't make it better and we both know that."

Lorene dropped her hose and came to stand by the car. "Alice, you need to work on your negative attitude. You've got to look at the bright side. Our house was spared. We're okay. And everybody in this town did what they could to help each other. What's wrong with someone else coming to help, too? We need some new ideas around here, or we'll keep on suffering. I just don't see what's wrong with that. And even though you went through the worst before, this is different. It's a little bit of hope. Real hope."

"I'm fresh out of hope," Alice countered, wondering how Lorene would feel if Jay had left her high and dry at the altar. But then, Jay Hobert was not that kind of man. He had integrity and he loved Lorene. Cranking the car, she waited for it to sputter to life then looked up into Lorene's disappointed face. "I'm sorry, Lo. I should be more like you, but I can't see the bright side of this."

Lorene leaned in close, as close as her growing stomach would let her. "Honey, he read your story. That means your words made a difference to someone, and this particular someone isn't a fly-by-night drifter out to do us in. Didn't you write that story so people would remember Bayou Rosette and all that our ancestors did to make this a good town, and to make people more aware that we're still alive and kicking around here?"

Alice looked out over the garden, remembering her parents sitting in the old swing, smiling and giggling. The yard was becoming dormant now, shutting down for fall and winter. She wished she could just shrink away and hibernate, too. Why was she being so stubborn about this? "Yes, I did write about our history to attract visitors. I just wanted people to see us, to notice us."

Lorene rested her hand on her stomach. "Well, somebody did. And I say more power to the man."

"Power—that's what scares me," Alice replied. Then she patted her sister's hand. "I've got to get to work. I'm sure Dotty will be all over this like a duck on a june bug. I might not like the man, but if anyone gets this story, it's gonna be me. I have to convince Dotty of that."

"You'll do it justice, I know," Lorene said. "You're always fair. Just try to have an open mind, okay?"

"Okay, all right," Alice said as she shifted into Reverse and backed the car out of the driveway. "I'll behave, I promise."

Lorene didn't look so sure. Alice had given her sister plenty of reason to doubt over the years since their parents had died in a car wreck out on the interstate. Alice had been thirteen, Lorene eighteen, when it had happened. They had clung together and refused to leave their home even though friends and relatives from around the state had offered them shelter. Lorene had finished high school, but instead of going to Tulane as she'd always dreamed, she had taken classes at a nearby community college so she could stay with Alice. Then she had worked it out so that a retired aunt could come and help out with Alice while Lorene worked at night at a local restaurant. Somehow, between the modest inheritance their parents had left and their combined work money, they'd managed to hang on to their house and land—even through a major storm and even through Alice's devastation after Ned Jackson's lies.

So much sacrifice. Lorene had worked at night to make extra money, just so they could keep Rosette House and so Alice could get the degree at Tulane that Lorene never had the chance to pursue. Between her scholarships and her own job, Alice had managed to get through college, but she came home the minute she graduated, armed with a journalism degree and a restless spirit. She didn't want to be anywhere else, she reminded herself now. She owed her sister so much.

Maybe she could try to change her attitude, for Lorene's sake, at least. And to remind herself that she'd come home hoping to make changes, hoping to create her own niche here in the place she loved.

What if Jonah Sheridan could help her do that? Would that be so wrong? Alice didn't have the same strong convictions as her sister. She prayed, same as Lorene, but she wasn't so sure her requests were always as pure as her sister's. But in spite of her doubts and her cynical nature, Alice still held out hope, too. She didn't like to admit that, but if she looked closely she knew she'd find a little glimmer of hope somewhere deep inside her bruised heart. How else could she have written that story only months after Ned had broken her heart? She wasn't so sure she was ready to nurture that hope, though.

"We need to follow up on this, Alice," Dotty Tillman said later that morning. "*You* need to follow up on this. So why are you sitting here?"

Alice lifted an eyebrow. "Are you suggesting I stalk the man, Dotty?"

Dotty stuck her pen into the thick auburn-colored bundle of wiry hair surrounding her café-au-lait face, then looked down through her pink bifocals. "Isn't that what a good reporter does?"

Alice was suddenly having doubts regarding her abilities to remain neutral about Jonah Sheridan. "But...by the time our story comes out next month, he might be long gone anyway."

Dotty again looked through her bifocals, a hand moving in the air. "Okay, kid, what's really going on? You come in here and tell me about this Jonah Sheridan person and how he's out to rebuild practically the whole town, but you don't have that enthusiasm I like in a reporter. In fact, you seem downright depressed about this scoop. Spill it, Alice."

Alice sank back in her chair then glanced out the front window of the tiny cottage where the *Bayou Buzz* offices were located on Bayou Drive. Everything around here seemed to have the word *bayou* in it, one way or another. Maybe because all the people around here had bayou blood running through their veins. She could see the Bayou Belle Inn across the square.

The blue Victorian house that had become an inn and restaurant over twenty years ago sat back from the road, surrounded by ancient live oaks and tall magnolias on the street side and bald cypress trees and trailing bougainvillea vines on the bayou side. Leaves from the nearby red oaks and tallow trees floated by in graceful symmetry each time the fall wind blew. Alice shivered, feeling that wind like a warning inside her soul.

"I guess I don't buy it," she finally admitted. "He just shows up one day all gung ho about a place he's never even seen before. I don't trust this man."

Dotty let out a huff of breath. "Suga', you don't trust any man, not since—"

"Don't remind me," Alice said, getting up to pace around the square office, where her own big desk behind the reception counter served as her home away from home. "I don't want to make the same mistake twice, Dotty. I vouched for Ned. I convinced people to hire him. And even though Jonah Sheridan seems like the real deal, I just can't get excited about this. Maybe I am being too negative, but it's hard right now."

Dotty dropped her glasses on Alice's desk. Her gold hoop earrings shimmied as she shook her head. "We all make mistakes, you know. Especially when it comes to men."

"Is that why you've never married?" Alice asked, hoping to glean a bit of information from her tight-lipped boss. No one really knew much about Dotty, except that she had grown up in Texas and lived in New Orleans until a few years ago. She'd started a multicultural magazine there, but something had gone wrong and she'd wound up here. A blessing for Alice, since she'd needed a job, but a mystery for the whole town. More fat to chew, more fodder for bayou legends. "Dotty?"

Dotty's exotic chocolate-colored eyes widened. "We were talking about you, kid, not me."

And that was as far as she usually got with lovable, stubborn, opinionated, exotic Dotty. No denial, no explanation. Dotty didn't talk about Dotty. But she lived to write the truth about everyone else.

"I'll get the story. You know that," Alice said, wishing Dotty would allow other human beings close. Her boss was a loner. And she never darkened the church doors. Dotty didn't seem to need God in her life. And that made Alice sad. And determined to help her friend and mentor.

"I want the story, no doubt," Dotty said, getting back to business. "But I want a good, solid story. Not just some notes and an attitude. Get to the bottom of this, Alice. Find out what's behind Jonah Sheridan's driving need to come to a town he'd never even visited and help us rebuild. Does he have some gold stashed away to help the poor and needy? Or does he have some other reason for wanting to do this? You need to find out, because we both know there's always more to the story."

"I will," Alice said, but her heart hammered like loose tin hitting against a barn roof, fast and steady. "I didn't say I had to like the man to get to the truth."

"No, you sure didn't," Dotty replied, her expression smug and sure. "You didn't have to. Apparently, our Mr. Sheridan got to you in a big way."

Alice shook her head. "No, he didn't. *He did not.* He just got my feathers ruffled with all his pie-in-the-sky talk."

"And maybe with his crisp brown hair and lady-killer smile?" Dotty asked, staring beyond where Alice stood with her back to the window. "Or maybe the way he walks all loose-limbed and laid-back?"

"You've seen him?" Alice wanted to bite her tongue. She'd just verified that she agreed with Dotty's spot-on description by blurting out the question.

"Yep," Dotty replied without missing a beat. "Up close, too."

"When?"

"About two minutes ago, when he started walking across the street toward our front door."

Alice whirled around in shock just as the man himself opened the door and looked up to find her staring at him.

Jonah's surprise caused him to inhale a deep breath. "Uh, hello, ladies." He could tell they'd been discussing *him,* since one looked guilty and the other one looked amused.

The guilty one—the one with the blond curls dancing around her high cheekbones—sank back against a cluttered desk. "What brings you to see us, Mr. Sheridan?"

"It's Jonah," he said, leaning against the tall receptionist's counter. "I came by to see if we could talk."

The amused one got up and came around the desk to extend her hand. "I'm sorry. Our receptionist is out on an errand. I'm Dotty Tillman, publisher and owner of the *Bayou*

Buzz. And you're just the man we wanted to see."

He smiled, thinking this was a very good sign. He'd thought about how to deal with Alice Bryson, and he'd decided to gain her trust before she decided to delve too heavily into him and his past and his future. He had to keep her close so she wouldn't dig too deep. "Great, because I wanted to see you, too." He shook Dotty's hand but he kept his eyes on Alice. "If you're not busy."

"We are," Alice said, folding her arms across her midsection in a hostile stance.

"We are not," Dotty replied as she cut her gaze to Alice. "Come on back and have a seat, Jonah. Maybe you can fill us in on all these rumors. Tell us a little bit more about your plans for this area."

Seeing the perturbed look on Alice's face, Jonah walked past her and settled down on a high-backed floral chair. "That's why I'm here, actually. I plan on giving the local weekly paper an interview, but I wanted to offer y'all the chance for an all-out, in-depth exclusive on this project. That way, your story will hit at just about the time we get things going on the property."

Dotty grinned big, her dark eyes beaming

with glee. "Funny, that's exactly what we were talking about. I just assigned Alice to cover you—I mean, to cover your project. I wanted her to find out all she could so our readers will get the big picture on this."

"I'm willing to allow that," Jonah replied. This was going better than he'd imagined. "I want y'all to understand the importance of this plan."

Alice didn't move. She didn't even seem to be breathing. She just stared at both of them as if she were caught in some sort of trap. And maybe he was entrapping her. She wanted a story and he wanted her approval. This seemed the best way toward achieving both.

"Alice, you heard the man," Dotty said. "So what's the plan, Jonah?"

He leaned forward, cupping his hands together. "I think it would be a good idea for Alice to shadow me while I'm here over the next few weeks." He met her heated gaze with a determined look. "I'll give you full access to my reports, my blueprints and my construction plans, then you can decide what kind of spin you want to put on the story."

"And you won't force me to sugarcoat it?"

"Not at all. I'm sure you'll be so impressed that you'll want to write a glowing report."

"Mighty confident, isn't he?" Dotty asked with a wink.

"Yes, mighty." Alice sliced him with her glare. "What's the name of your project?"

Surprised at that question coming out of the blue, he said, "I haven't really given it a name yet. I wanted to come down here first, get a feel for things."

"Uh-huh. And what are you feeling so far?"

Jonah couldn't answer that question right now. Because he was certainly feeling things he'd never experienced before with any other woman—a sense of confusion, a little bit of awe and admiration, and a whole lot of attraction. He swallowed, noticed the room had grown quiet and warm. "I want to name this development something unique and different, something meaningful. I guess it'll come to me sooner or later."

"I need to know what to call it—for the article," Alice replied, obviously oblivious to the buzz of electricity that seemed to hiss through the air around them. "And right now, I'm feeling either Pipe Dream or Scam City. How does that sound?"

"Alice!" Dotty's shrill voice broke the tension in the room. "Do you want this story or not, 'cause I can assign it to Scooter if you don't."

Alice scowled at Dotty. "Scooter? He's an intern. He couldn't do this story justice if it came to him complete in a dream."

"Exactly. But he might have a more professional attitude, if you get my drift."

Jonah was getting her drift, all right. Dotty looked as tough as nails in spite of her bright-colored, abstract silk blouse and pink fingernail polish. But Alice seemed every bit as formidable in her white sweater and blue button-up shirt and crisp khaki work pants. Coupled with that chip on her shoulder, of course.

"I'm sorry," Alice said, looking contrite. "I'll do the story," she added, her blue eyes tinged with fire. "But I want all the details, everything. I owe it to the people of this town to give them the truth. And I do mean the whole truth."

"You've got it," Jonah said, reaching out to shake her hand. "I've got nothing to hide." At least work-wise, he had nothing to hide.

Alice took his hand and gripped it with all the strength of a vise. "Don't make me regret this," she told him, squeezing his fingers together, her smile so pretty no one would know she was trying to cut off the circulation to his arm.

"You won't regret it," he promised with a prayer. After Alice released his hand, he said, "I'll show you I have good intentions."

Dotty stood up. "Okay then, we have four weeks until we go to print. Let's get cracking."

Jonah stood and shook out his fingers. "When do you want to get started?" he asked Alice.

"Now's as good a time as any," she said. "Let's start with those reports and plans you mentioned."

Jonah nodded. "Want to meet me over at the Bayou Belle Café? I'll buy lunch."

"I'll be there in five minutes," she said, her look sweeping over him with a dare. "And I'm always prompt."

"I'll be waiting."

He nodded to Dotty—who was still very amused—then stepped out into the glaring fall sunshine. Why did it feel as if he'd just been handed a sentence to be executed?

But when he glanced back through the big window and saw Alice staring out at him with that deadly blue intent in her big eyes, he understood. He was afraid of how this woman made him feel—threatened and exposed and...longing for something he couldn't have. He was about to share his hopes and dreams with her. And she was all geared up to stomp them flat with her bitterness and her distrust of men coming to town bearing hope. He didn't need that kind of distraction on top of all the others things he had to deal with right now.

Telling himself to stop being defensive, Jonah vowed to stand his ground. His plan was solid and he needed to concentrate on that. His personal reasons for being here weren't part of the deal and his life wasn't any of Alice Bryson's business. He'd stick to the plan and be professional, show her this was a win-win situation and he'd get the job done.

And in the meantime, he'd hoped he'd be able to find out more about his real mother. Which left him wondering if *he'd* wind up being the one to regret this.

Chapter Four

The Bayou Belle Café was buzzing with the lunch crowd. The curious lunch crowd.

"We probably should have stayed at the magazine office and ordered in," Alice said on a winded whisper as she settled into the booth with Jonah. "People are staring."

"Maybe they're shocked to see you with me."

Alice shot him with a lengthy look. "What's that supposed to mean?"

His expression went from smiling to red-faced. "I mean, maybe they've heard already that you don't like me."

Now it was her turn to be embarrassed. "I never said I didn't like you. I said I don't trust you."

"Same difference."

"No, I like you just fine so far. I just don't know how I feel about this elaborate plan you have for my town."

"I'll show you my plans after we eat. I'm starving."

She looked him over. "You seem healthy enough. Looks like you get enough to eat, at least."

"Is that required in men you don't trust?"

His grin saved her from hitting him with a scathing retort. "Okay, I guess I've been a little antisocial with you. And you're probably right about folks—they'd be shocked to see me with any new man in town. I'm a jilted bride."

He tried to look surprised, but his expression didn't quite make it in time to rescue the traces of sympathy and concern in his eyes. "I'm sorry to hear that." Even his comment was lame and pathetic. Or maybe she was the pathetic one.

Alice shook her head. "And don't even tell me you had no idea. I love Jimmy and Paulette like family but they sure love to gossip."

"They just like to make small talk with their customers."

"Yeah, lots of small talk about big things—such as me standing in a white dress in my backyard, watching the man I thought I was going to marry driving away. He got the impression I was gonna call the police on him."

"Why didn't you—I mean, if he did the things I've heard he did?"

"I didn't tell him, but I'd already reported him to the local authorities minutes before we were supposed to get married," Alice replied, memories moving through her mind with the crackling intensity of those falling leaves outside the big window.

Somehow, Jonah knowing all the intimate details of her sad life didn't bother her as much as she would have thought. Had she become that numb to feeling things, or was she just glad someone else had spared her the humiliation of telling him herself?

"I told Ned the wedding was off and if he didn't get out of town, I'd call the sheriff. My brother-in-law, Jay, backed me up on that and then we watched him leave. But Ned was long gone by the time the sheriff got out to our house and we haven't seen hide or hair of him since. But he'll mess up one day. He's a wanted man now and justice will prevail."

"I sure hope so." Jonah smiled up at the waitress. "I'll have the Jimmy burger with all the works. And for the lady—?" He glanced over at Alice. "What would you like?"

Alice greeted the waitress then said, "I'll have the Cobb salad and iced tea."

He waited until they were alone again. "I really am sorry about what happened to you. But I'm not a con artist. I came here with a whole different set of goals than those of your runaway groom. Will you hear me out?"

Alice watched his face, wondering if her scam-radar was working correctly. The man seemed genuinely passionate about his work. And the way his eyes had grazed over her just now with such a hungry eagerness made her think she might have misjudged him.

"I'm willing to withhold judgment so I can get the best story," she finally said. "I'll be objective in the article, but that doesn't mean I have to agree with you."

"Fair enough." Jonah unrolled the subdivision plans. "This is the first phase."

She shifted on her seat. "You intend to have more than one phase in this thing?"

He nodded. "If all goes as planned, sure." His gray eyes widened. "There's a lot of land for sale around here. The families who left here after the hurricane aren't going to come back when they don't have anything to come back to. But I hope to market this as a good retirement place, near New Orleans and within easy access to all the major interstates. Small-town living near the big city."

"What if the neighbors who lived around the bend *do* want to come back? Several houses were either blown completely away or torn down. Do they have a choice?"

"They have that choice. I'm only buying when lots are available and when I can buy land in volume."

"You mean you're not coercing people to sell?"

"No. I don't operate that way."

She wondered about that, but she had to stay objective. "Okay, since I'm going to be neutral with this story, I'll just pretend that I believe you, for now."

He leaned across the table then flipped the plans around. "Let me explain this and then you can take it back to the office and study it. I've got several sets so take your time. I'd like your opinion—and not just for a good story. I'd really like to know what you think."

That surprised her. Was he trying to flatter her to win points or did the man honestly want the truth? "*My* opinion? Why?"

"Don't look so doubtful. You live here and

it's obvious you care what happens to the bayou. I need someone to tell me if I'm on the right track—the style of the cottages, the size of the lots, what kind of trees and landscaping to plant. That sort of thing. I want this to be as natural and pretty as possible while still being environmentally sound. The homes will be energy efficient but comfortable. I want each one to be unique—not just cooker-cutter type houses."

Alice glanced over the graphs and charts and construction plans. "It was pretty and natural and unique before the storms came. I'd sure like to see that again." She tapped a finger on the papers. "And even though I kind of denied it the other day, I'd like to have neighbors again, people I can get to know and socialize with. We used to have crawfish boils on the bayou, Christmas festivals right here on this main street with a big bonfire on the bayou, and we always celebrated Memorial Day and the Fourth of July with a lot of parties and get-togethers, and lots of fireworks." She glanced out the window. "Sometimes, it seems like a ghost town out there. We've tried to bring all of that back, but I don't think people have the heart for it the way they did before."

She shrugged. "Don't get me wrong, those of us who were born and raised here feel strongly about this place and we celebrate, regardless of the past. But…something is missing. It's like our heart is broken." And she should know. Her heart *was* broken. Broken by lost dreams and empty promises, broken from grief and a hopeless feeling that ached inside her soul.

"I want to change that," he said, his fingers brushing against her hand as he started rolling the papers back together. "And I need your help to do that." He tapped one of the house plans. "I'm going to start by building a model cottage right away so I just want to warn you about that. I haven't quite finished the plans for that one, but I hope to get some inspiration while I'm here."

Alice took a sip of her tea. "Maybe I'll get some inspiration, too. I need to be more positive about rebuilding this community."

He lifted his chin in agreement. "I understand. If things don't go well, I'll sell the model and move on. But…I'm hoping people will respond and we'll be selling lots of land and houses in the coming months. And after that, new business should crop up to support the new citizens moving to this area."

Alice still didn't trust him, but he looked earnest enough sitting there with that determined, almost dreamy expression on his handsome face. But that didn't mean she was ready to give him a full-fledged endorsement. "I'll help by giving everyone my honest observations in the article, stating both the pros and cons of this venture. That's all I can offer for now. Take it or leave it," Alice added with a shrug as their food arrived.

"I'll take it," he replied, his eyes crinkling enough to give her a good view of the crow's-feet etched around them. Had he gotten those crow's-feet from laughing or from life in general? And why did that make him so endearing to her?

"Just don't make me regret this."

"Never."

When she looked up at him, he'd gone all serious, his eyes a dark, churning gray now, and full of such a sweet sincerity she almost regretted being so gruff and mean to him. He did seem a likable person and he wasn't bad to look at—all suntanned and rugged and boyish.

Almost. She *almost* regretted not trusting him. But *almost* didn't make things right. She'd almost been married. Her parents had almost made it home. And almost regretting things didn't make life any better.

She was tired of almost. She wanted for sure. She wanted certainty and she wanted a blessed assurance that this time things would truly be better. But how could she expect a man she'd just met to give her all that she longed for? Jonah had come here on some sort of mission—whether from a creative need to fulfill dreams or maybe just with the need to make things happen, she couldn't be sure. But who was she to question his motives, to stomp on his dreams and his goals, just because her own had gone south?

"What's your impression so far?" he asked between bites of his Jimmy burger.

"So far, I think you have a very good plan and I hope it works. But we'll have to see about all of this, Jonah. I'll set up appointments with the mayor and the chamber president to get their views, and I'll talk to a lot of the locals. When's the town meeting?"

"In a couple of days. You'll need to be there."

"Oh, I will be, just as I promised. And I'll probably have a lot of questions for you then, too."

"I'd expect nothing less."

They ate in silence for a while then she

said, "Why is my opinion so important? Is it because I'm a reporter? Or is it because you think I can sway people, or is it both? Or is it maybe because I'm the first person to question you and you like a good challenge? You hope to win me over out of sheer stubborn pride?"

"Do you always analyze to this degree?"

"I'm a reporter. It's part of the job."

He finished a crisp Cajun fry then sipped his soda. He looked right into her eyes. "It's because you're you, Alice. You *are* opinionated and stubborn, but those traits mean you'll also be honest with me—brutally honest."

"And you like that in a woman?"

He leaned close then, his eyes twinkling like lights on dark water. "I like it in *you,* that's for sure. But then I've liked you since I read your article. And I've read it several times since I saw the reprint in that paper. I told you, you're the main reason I came down here. I think you're my inspiration and that's not just a line."

She pushed her plate away then sank back on the booth's puffed red vinyl, holding back the urge to laugh in his face. "Or maybe you just think since I got burned once by a charmer with big dreams that you need to really work on me to make me believe in you, so you can get on with business and build your little bayou community."

She wasn't prepared for the flash of fire shining in his eyes. Or the intensely serious expression settling over his features. "You can go right on thinking that all you want, Alice, but you might as well know one thing about me—I don't back down when I want something. And not even a blonde with pretty blue eyes can make me change my mind on this project. I want you to believe in me, yes. But I'm not going to jump through hoops for you. I'll be honest and up-front with you and I'll try my best to prove that I'm the real deal. After that, your opinion won't matter very much. But I'll still value it. So get over the notion that I'm using you for evil gain, okay? In fact, get over the notion that this is all about you. It's not. It's about helping people who need help. And we've all been there before."

With that, he got up, threw a twenty on the table and offered her his hand. "I've got work to do and I'm sure you can't wait to find the flaws in my work plans, so let's get out of here."

Alice gulped the last of her tea, too shocked to respond to his biting comeback.

And too full of pride to admit she had it coming. Her mother always warned her that her smarty attitude would do her in.

She was just being cautious now, which meant she had to have a bit of attitude. Even if Jonah's words did cut to the bone.

"Thanks for lunch," she managed to mutter as they walked out into the crisp fall afternoon. "I'll see you at the town meeting."

"I'll be looking for you," he said, his tone subdued. "In the meantime, you have an open invitation to follow me around and listen in on anything I have to say."

"I'll get back to you on that."

She needed time to digest all the many facets of Jonah Sheridan. And to do some research on the man, too.

She was either selling him short or he had her fooled.

And she wouldn't be fooled again.

Chapter Five

Jonah stared down at the documents in front of him. He'd come to the small library to research the local history a little more and to maybe find out some information on his biological mother. All he had to go on was a name—Esther Mayeaux. But that was her maiden name and so far, even though he'd found information on the Mayeaux who'd lived here, he hadn't found any traces of anyone named Esther. When he got a chance he'd have to go to the parish courthouse and search the public records. But he had to handle this very carefully. He didn't want to lose focus on his work or get any more rumors started.

"How's it going?"

He looked up to find the bubbly gray-haired librarian smiling down at him. "Not as well as I'd hoped," he said, noting from her name tag that her name was Betty Nell Hollis.

Her eyebrows lifted. "Is this research for your new community?"

He smiled, resigning himself to the fact that nothing was secret around here. "Kinda. I'm just digging into some of the local history."

Betty glanced at the books and documents scattered around the table. "Lot of old family names in those pages. Lots of solid history. You know, Cajuns are famous for their storytelling abilities."

"So I've heard." He decided to ask Betty Nell some questions, but first he qualified his curiosity. "I'm a history buff, so I'm glad someone recorded the history of Bayou Rosette. But I'd sure like to find out more, maybe talk to some folks."

She nodded. "I know a lot of old-timers who might be willing to talk to you."

"Do you remember the Mayeaux family?"

She looked surprised and then nodded. "Oh, yeah. Those Mayeaux brothers were always in trouble."

Brothers? He didn't dare ask her about Esther. He'd do a little more digging on his own. "Do you know anyone who might be able to help me fill in the blanks on some of the families who lived along the bayou, including the Mayeaux?"

"Have you talked to Alice Bryson?"

He laughed. "Oh, yeah. But I need someone who's a little older than she is."

Betty Nell pursed her lips. "You might try Arnold Gauthier out on the old River Road. He's our local storyteller and poet. He knows everything about everybody on this bayou, but I'll warn you he's old and ornery and he can't always remember as accurately as you might like."

Jonah tried to act nonchalant. "Thanks. That might be my next step." Looking at his watch, he got up. "I'm sorry. You're waiting for me to leave so you can close, aren't you?"

Betty Nell grinned. "Take your time. I'm just going home to sit in front of the television." Her grin faded and so did the brightness in her eyes. "My husband passed away last year, so it's just me and the cat now."

"I'm sorry," Jonah said again, gathering up documents and some old self-published histories he'd found. "I've always been a loner myself, but I imagine it's hard to be alone after being married for a long time."

"Forty-two years for us," she said, her eyes soft with memories. "I have children and grandchildren but they all live far away. I get to see them once or twice a year."

Jonah took that in. "Where do you live?"

She shook a thumb toward the door. "About a mile from here in a trailer on the bayou."

Jonah couldn't say that was very near where he planned to build. "Did you lose your house in the storm?"

She inclined her chin. "Yes." He watched as she swallowed then blinked. "I think that's why I lost my John, too. He never quite got over it." She took some of the documents he'd gathered. "And truth be told, that's why my kids don't come to visit much. No room and too depressing." Then she looked over at him, her eyes misty. "Mister, if you're here to rebuild, I say more power to you. I might not be able to afford one of your houses, but I'd sure love to see some of these young families in good, solid homes. It's too late for me, I reckon, but they deserve better."

Jonah's heart beat with renewed commitment. He touched his hand to Betty Nell's. "I'll explain everything at the town meeting, but just between you and me, Miss Betty Nell, I'm about to make you a promise."

She looked both hopeful and doubtful. "What's that, son?"

"I promise you'll be in one of my houses by this time next year."

"You can't make that kind of promise," she said, tears springing up in her eyes. "No one can."

Jonah picked up his briefcase. "I just did and when I make a promise, I don't forget it." He reached out to shake her hand. "Do you believe me?"

Betty Nell took his hand and he felt the tremors in her grip. "I'd like to believe you. But I can't afford to go along on false hope."

She sounded a lot like Alice. This town needed real hope. Jonah prayed to that end that he might be the one to offer it. And it occurred to him that it had been a long time since he'd sent up an earnest prayer. But this one was earnest *and* urgent. He wanted it to happen.

"I won't let you down," he said, smiling over at her. "Just wait and see."

She watched him as he headed for the door, her old eyes bright and misty. "I'll see you around, then."

"I'll be back to check out some more history books," he said, waving goodbye.

After the door shut, Betty Nell finished

picking up the books off the table, then called out to her last customer. "You can come out now, Alice. He's gone."

Alice slinked around a stout bookshelf and stared across the tidy room at Betty Nell. "Do you believe him?"

Betty Nell shrugged. "I've gone about as low as a person can go and still have hope, honey. So yes, I think I do believe him. I'm gonna try to believe him because I've prayed for some sort of new beginning. And that's not easy for an old lady. But God doesn't always allow the easy way out. When we walk the hard road, we usually find our way home. And it's all the more sweet because of the journey."

Alice pushed at her curls, thinking Betty Nell should have been a writer instead of a librarian. She had such a way with being philosophical and smart. Alice had always considered herself to be a professional, but apparently she could only come up with odd and alarming ways to get her stories these days.

She'd been sneaky and secretive with this particular subject, eavesdropping behind a bookshelf. But it had happened by accident. She'd come hopping through the shortcut from her office to the library, taking the back entrance just as she'd done a hundred times before, only to look up the hallway and see Jonah sitting there absorbed in a big history book.

And she'd panicked. Yes, she was supposed to be shadowing the man, but he hadn't called today and she hadn't found the courage to call him since their lunch had ended so abruptly yesterday. So she'd taken care of some other business around the office and set up times to interview other sources for the story. It wasn't her fault that he'd been sitting there in the library and hadn't noticed her in the dark back hallway. She'd done the only thing she could—she'd hidden behind one of the shelves and put a finger to her lips to warn Betty Nell away.

Not so she could eavesdrop, but just so she could find what she needed and leave, quietly and quickly, before she got into another round of banter with the man.

And it surely wasn't her fault that she'd heard him talking to Betty Nell. But it *was* his fault that he'd almost made her cry with his kindness and consideration.

Almost. He'd almost made her cry. Had he made a blind promise to a lonely old woman, or did he mean to make good on that pledge?

Alice looked at Betty Nell, so diligent, so steady and devoted, and hoped with all her heart that Jonah did live up to that bold declaration.

Because if he didn't, Alice would make sure he paid dearly for it. It was one thing to make promises to her, but quite another to toy with the hopes of someone as good and solid as Betty Nell Hollis.

She walked up to the check-out desk. "I hope he comes through for you, Betty Nell. I truly do."

Betty Nell gave her a soft smile. "Sometimes, prayers are answered, suga'. But not always in the way we expect."

Alice thought about that and wondered if her own prayers were being answered. She'd often asked God to help her town, to help the people she loved. And to help her, too, to get over her bitterness and her doubts.

Had He sent Jonah to do just that?

She took a breath, giving it over to God for now.

And then she remembered something Jonah had asked Betty Nell. "I wonder why he wanted to know about the Mayeaux family."

"He's a history buff," Betty Nell said. "I

think he's interested in anyone who lived on the bayou."

"But why that particular family?" Alice asked, her radar detector going on full alert. "The way I remember it from hearing my parents talk, the Mayeaux gave the Brysons a really hard time throughout the years."

Betty Nell slanted her head. "They did live here years ago and yes, they were bad neighbors. Very bad. But they all left long ago." She leaned close. "I've heard things over the years, but…I'm not one to pass gossip."

Alice thought Betty Nell was the only person in this town who didn't pass gossip. "Yes, I remember my daddy talking about them. But that was so many years ago that very few outsiders would even remember them. So why does Jonah want to know about them?"

"I think he's probably heard a lot about all the local characters," Betty Nell explained. "He also looked over the picture book of Rosette House, but then he told me he'd read your article regarding that, too. I told him to go talk to Arnold Gauthier, but we both know that old man doesn't like people coming up onto his property. I probably should have warned Jonah about that."

Alice grinned. "He'll find out soon

enough." Mr. Arnold was about as ornery and obstinate as a gnarled gator, but he did know a lot about the people of this town, both past and present, and he still lived in a little shack out past the curve of the bayou.

She had to wonder if Jonah might pay Mr. Arnold a visit. Which meant Alice would also pay him a visit.

To find out why Jonah was so interested in the notorious Mayeaux family.

Jonah stood across from the weathered cabin, his heart tapping a beat like a woodpecker hitting a tree trunk. Would Mr. Gauthier talk to him? He'd heard the man was a recluse. A recluse with a shotgun, from what Jimmy had told him when he'd asked for directions.

But Jonah needed to see the man, so he walked from the dirt lane up to the creaking porch, then knocked on the front door.

He heard shuffling sounds inside. "Who's dat?"

Jonah had to strain to make out the words. "I'm Jonah Sheridan, Mr. Gauthier. I wanted to talk to you about the history around here. I have some questions about the families who lived on the bayou and I was told you were the local authority."

"Don't talk to strangers, me."

Jonah held two fingers to his forehead, doing an automatic massage as he tried to find another angle. "I'm in town to help rebuild some of the houses along the bayou. I'd like to talk to you about the history so I can build the houses according to tradition. I want these houses to be special, to—"

He didn't get to finish. The old wooden door fell back on its rusted hinges then settled with a bang against the slats of the wall. For a few seconds there was only silence and dust balls, then Arnold Gauthier emerged from the shadows, his dark eyes wild, his brows bushy and gray, his hair and beard both long and shaggy and rusty-white. He wore overalls and a button-up cotton shirt and…he was holding a shotgun.

Jonah listened to a long string of Cajun-French, not sure if he wanted to know the translation. Then Arnold Gauthier said, "Either you real crazy or just plain stupid to come here and knock on my door like dis. But…me, I believe in keeping the past and I especially have a soft spot for this old swamp." Then he grinned, showing aged teeth. "And dat's about the only reason you still alive, monsieur." Then he let out a hoot of laughter. "Get you on in here, son. We pass the time a bit, yes?"

"Yes," Jonah said as he let out a breath. "Yes. I'd like that. I'd like that very much."

Alice drove by the dirt lane twice before parking her car and walking up the road. All around her, bugs of various sizes and shapes buzzed and swarmed in the lush foliage and the overgrown bushes, but she swatted at them and kept on going. When she came around the bend in the rutted road, she saw Jonah's sleek navy pickup parked in the yard next to Mr. Gauthier's rusted-out Chevy truck. The shiny new vehicle looked out of place amongst the eclectic iron and wood sculptures and spoon-and-fork wind chimes that dotted the yard and the trees.

So he was in there right now talking to Arnold Gauthier. That gained Jonah points, at least. People rarely got past the ancient live oaks, let alone into the cabin itself. Arnold was friendly enough but the man liked his privacy. A lot. So why had he let Jonah inside? And why had it been so important to Jonah to talk to Arnold?

This had to be about more than just a stroll

down memory lane. Jonah needed information from the local historian. And Arnold didn't give out information without a very good reason. What was that reason? What was going on?

Did she dare knock on the door and ask?

Or should she just turn around and run back up the lane and go home before both dusk and bugs descended down on her?

Deciding she hadn't sunk so low that she'd intrude on an old man she respected, Alice decided to turn around. She'd confront Jonah later, maybe call him to meet with her tonight after supper. But she had to know. She wanted to trust him but already he was sneaking around, hiding from her.

She got in her car, then sat staring at the woods and the trees, thinking maybe she was being unfair. He hadn't actually been sneaking around. He'd told her she could follow him, right? And she hadn't bothered calling him this morning. That was her fault and her problem if Dotty found out.

She could tell Jonah that Betty Nell had mentioned this visit as a possible source of information, which was true. But would he buy that she only wanted to listen in, or would he think she was spying on him?

"I'm *supposed* to be spying on him, sorta," she told herself as she drove back toward Rosette House. "That's my job. So why am I being so defensive?" And why wasn't she doing what she usually did with a story—gathering background information, doing her homework, getting together sources and facts. She had to snap out of this morose attitude and get on with things.

She'd call the man. She'd find out what was going on.

Maybe he just needed logical explanations regarding the history of the bayou. But building houses didn't demand much from the past, did it? He did say he loved history and he'd told Betty Nell that was the reason he wanted to talk to some of the local old-timers. Or was Jonah Sheridan here for more than just building houses and studying the local history? Did he have some sort of connection to the Mayeaux clan? Is that why he'd bought the acreage across from Rosette House?

Her gut instincts told her he had another reason for rebuilding this community. But what was that reason? If anyone could find out the truth, it would be her, Alice decided. With that thought in mind, she headed up the stairs to her apartment, hoping her nosy sister wouldn't call her for a report of the day's activities.

The phone was ringing when she unlocked the door.

Chapter Six

"I'll be down later for tea, I promise."

"No, that won't do," Lorene said in a prim tone. "You have to come for dinner."

Alice closed her eyes and counted to ten. Why did Lorene act like a mother hen? "I can't come for dinner. I have some work to do. But tea later would be good."

"Dinner," Lorene replied. "You have to. I invited a guest."

Alice groaned out loud. "You know how I feel about blind dates, Lo."

"This isn't a blind date," her sister said. "You know this man."

Alice tossed down her laptop bag, a sudden sense of doom darkening her mind. Overdramatic, she knew, but it described the feelings coursing through her system. "Who is it?"

"Jonah Sheridan."

She wanted to scream but she held the scream inside, opting to question her sister's sanity instead. "Are you crazy? Why would you go and do a thing like that?"

Lorene chuckled. "He called here just a few minutes ago, looking for you. He'd tried both your cell and your apartment phone. Said he was trying to gather as many sources as possible on the history of Bayou Rosette. He wants to tour Rosette House and he wanted you to be here when he does it. I told him you'd be home soon and why didn't he come tonight for dinner."

"Well, aren't you just Miss Hospitality." Alice slumped in a high-backed chair, then put one hand on the old, round oak table she'd lovingly restored last year. Her cell was off and she just now saw the blinking light on her answering machine. Avoidance tactics, maybe? "And you know I can't say no, or I'll look like a bad-mannered brat. Why do you do these things to me?"

"I didn't do anything but think logically," Lorene replied. "I have plenty of fresh, homemade bread and crawfish bisque and the man seemed impatient to ask some questions. I can't think on an empty stomach and you need to eat, don't you?"

"I'm not that hungry. *Now.*"

"Just get down here and help me make a salad," Lorene said. Then Alice heard the solid flat-line of the dial tone.

"Yes, ma'am." She threw the phone receiver down, then saluted her sister through the walls.

At least she might be able to ask Jonah how things had gone with Mr. Gauthier. Just seeing his reaction would be worth sitting through an awkward dinner, she decided. And sooner or later, she had to do her job, whether she wanted to or not. She'd done a lot of behind-the-scenes research on his company, at least. JS Building and Development was a solid company, all right. The man had managed to build a small empire in the last few years. But she wanted to find out more.

What's holding me back, Lord? Why did she have this sense of dread regarding Jonah? Maybe because he was handsome and interesting and he seemed sincere. And maybe because she wasn't ready to give any man credit for those admirable traits right now. She didn't want to like Jonah. She didn't want to trust him, either. She wanted to stew in her self-pity just a bit more. Only, that was silly and a real waste of time. She could sit through a dinner with him, at least.

She looked at the clock and almost didn't freshen up. Almost. But on a feminine whim, she whirled and headed for the bright, white bathroom, longing for a soothing soak in the big claw-foot tub she'd found in an antique shop in New Orleans. Standing over the gleaming white, old-fashioned pedestal sink, Alice stared in the ornate, gold-etched mirror, deciding her unruly curls couldn't be fixed.

"All frizz in this humidity, as usual," she said on a loud fume of breath. With a defiant grunt, she shoved most of her curls up and clasped them on top of her head with an industrial-strength silver clip, then brushed her teeth and put on some pink gloss and fresh blush. She changed out of her work clothes into a flowing, lightweight sweater and comfortable old jeans. A quick spray of floral perfume and she was out the door.

And ready to face Jonah Sheridan.

He stared across the dinner table at her, the delicious food in front of him growing cold. Why did Alice Bryson push all his buttons this way? Could it be the soft teal-green sweater that only highlighted her eyes, or was it the way she'd pulled her hair up in a haphazard but definitely attractive topknot? No, it was more the way she glanced at him when she thought he wasn't looking. It had to be the way she sat quietly eating her food, the intensity of her thoughts causing her brow to scrunch up. Or maybe it was the way she tore into the delicious fresh bread, then dabbed a bit more butter across the crispy brown crust.

He sure needed to get over any notions of a flirtation with Alice Bryson. He never let down his guard with women. He lived for work and worked to keep the blank spots in his life at bay. And maybe deep down inside, he wished he'd never come across Alice's article about this place. It had stirred up too many long dormant dreams, dreams he'd tried to put to rest. Now he was in turmoil, trying to balance work with personal strife.

"More salad, Jonah?"

He looked away from Alice to find her sister smiling at him with bright, all-seeing green eyes. "No, thanks. I'm good. The bisque is delicious."

Jay spoke up. "We always freeze some crawfish for the winter—just so Lorene can make her bisque. Wait till you try her crawfish dressing—beats regular turkey and dressing any day. And she makes it every Thanksgiving."

"I've never heard of that kind of dressing," Jonah said, wondering if he'd still be around for Thanksgiving. Wishing he could be here for the holiday, he scanned Alice again for any reaction to that notion.

She seemed overly interested in her bread.

"We like to eat around here," Lorene said, grinning. Then she patted her stomach. "Wow, somebody is sure energetic tonight."

"Did the baby kick?" Jay asked, his tone soft and intimate as he gazed at his glowing wife.

She nodded then sent him a shy smile. "I think it was a kick. He's been kind of quiet for the last few days. Maybe it was more of a pain—indigestion or something."

Jay's soft smile changed to a look of concern. "Are you sure?"

"I'm fine," Lorene replied, her words bringing Alice's head up. "I'm okay, really. Stop worrying, both of you." She leaned over to give her husband a reassuring peck on the cheek.

Jonah felt as if he were watching a love story on a big screen. And something in the watching made him ache for the same such scene in his own life. Which only caused him to look up at Alice again. And wonder.

She gave him a tight-lipped look, her blue eyes wide with a question. For a minute, he thought she might be feeling the same way. They'd had a nice, civil discussion before dinner on the history surrounding Bayou Rosette, mostly about Rosette House itself. Now he knew a little bit more about two of the original families who'd settled here. He wanted to ask Lorene and Alice if they knew anything about the Mayeaux family or about the ancient feud Mr. Gauthier had told him about. A feud between the Mayeaux and the Brysons, according to Mr. Gauthier's scanty recollections. Maybe Alice would be able to help him some on that without him having to tell her his real reasons for wanting information. But her next words dashed that brief hope.

"What were you doing at Mr. Gauthier's place today?" she said, her question echoing in the silence. And it was just a bit accusatory, even if she did have a sweet smile on her face.

Surprised, Jonah almost choked on the sip of tea he'd just taken. "How did you know I was there?"

"I'm a reporter, remember? I hear things." She shrugged. "And see things."

"Yeah, right." He wondered if she had indeed been "shadowing" him all day. And what else had she heard?

Lorene dropped her spoon. "Alice, what on earth are you talking about? Mr. Gauthier doesn't let people onto his property."

"Well, he did today. I saw Jonah there."

"You *were* following me, then," Jonah said, feeling both triumph and trepidation.

"Yes, I drove by and checked," she admitted, seemingly not in the least ashamed or embarrassed.

He had to give her credit for being honest, but he knew her well enough by now to know she wasn't telling him everything. "You can't just drive by that place. If you saw me there then you must have snuck up to the house."

She leaned forward, tenting her fingers, her elbows hitting the table. "What if I did?"

"That's not very professional, is it?"

Her smile actually looked serene. "I wasn't actually working at the time. I was just curious."

He smiled back, polite but firm. "Oh, I get it. You wanted to catch me doing something sneaky?"

"Alice, pass me the butter," Lorene said, her voice full of warning.

Alice slid the pristine crystal butter dish across the Battenburg lace tablecloth toward her sister, but her eyes stayed squarely on Jonah.

"Arnold Gauthier? Is that man still alive?" Jay asked, a hint of amused curiosity in his question.

"He was very alive today, but I'm surprised Jonah still is," Alice answered. "Did you two have a good talk?"

Jonah dropped his white linen napkin, his face fixed in his own fake smile. "As a matter of fact, we sure did. He told me a lot of things about this town, things that will help me get a handle on the kind of community I'm rebuilding. Good things and bad things."

"About the whole town or just the Mayeaux family?"

Jonah's pulse throbbed like a toothache, jarring his whole system. He liked this woman but she'd gone too far, messing in his personal business. "About both, actually. It's all part of the history. Just like this house and your land is part of the history."

"The Mayeaux family?" Lorene looked from Jonah to Alice, then back at her silent husband. "They were trouble from the get-go, according to my daddy. They never did like any of our relatives and they caused our parents some worries, too. I was real young, but I was relieved they moved away. Why do you want to know about them, anyway?"

"That's what I'd like to hear," Alice said, her arms now crossed over her stomach. "Why don't you tell us what you learned from Mr. Gauthier, Jonah?"

Jonah turned to Lorene. "I did talk to Mr. Gauthier about the Mayeaux family. He said they'd all left years ago, but he also told me they had a hard time and struggled to make ends meet. I'm going to find out more before I pass judgment."

Alice leaned forward, her interest obvious. "Why would you want to know about them? What does that have to do with building houses?"

"I want to get a complete picture of life in this area," he said. A poor excuse, but the only one he could come up with right now. And because he didn't want to discuss it anymore, he got up. "I enjoyed dinner, but I think it's time for me to leave."

"But what about the tour of the house?" Lorene asked, trying to stand.

"Some other time, maybe," Jonah replied. "Thanks again."

He gave Alice one last look. "Next time, just call me and that way you won't have to spy on me without my knowledge." Then he headed for the double French doors leading out to the front yard and he didn't bother looking back.

Even when he heard one of the doors banging open behind him.

"Jonah, wait!"

Alice watched as he stalked toward his car, wondering why she had to be so blunt and bullish at times. She certainly hadn't planned to ambush him that way but…she needed to know, to understand. She couldn't tolerate sneaking around or deceptive business practices. Not ever again.

He was simply visiting an old man who liked to reminisce about the past, she reminded herself as she hurried toward his car. Maybe she'd overreacted. "Are you going to leave then, just like that?"

"Yep." He got in, then stared out the window at her.

She knocked on the glass, thinking she should just let him go. But the look he'd given her in there shattered all of her resolve and made her want to explain. "Jonah, listen to me."

He finally let down the window. "I don't have to listen to you because you certainly don't listen to me. I told you I didn't mind you hanging out with me, Alice. But I do mind you sneaking around trying to make something sinister out of something normal. I'm a historian. I love history and I like to get all the historical facts on a place before I build houses. But I've told you all of this already. And even though your family apparently had a long-standing problem with the Mayeaux from way back when, it's especially important to me to get the facts straight about Bayou Rosette—the good and the bad."

"Why?" she said, putting her hands on her hips. "Why is it so very important? I still don't get why you came here and why you're so intent on doing this. I mean, you could rebuild in New Orleans or Biloxi or Bay Saint Louis, even Waveland. We weren't the only town affected by the hurricanes."

He looked out into the night then back at her. "But—"

She didn't get to hear what he might have said. Jay's frantic shout stopped Jonah's next words.

"Alice, come inside. I think Lorene's going into labor. Hurry!"

Alice's gaze hit Jonah as a sick feeling coated her stomach. "She's not due for another month."

Jonah jumped out of the car, all his anger seeming to disappear like a bayou mist. "C'mon. Let's go see what's wrong." He took her by the arm, leading her back to the house.

Alice didn't try to pull away. The warmth of his hand on her skin made her feel better. She didn't understand why being near Jonah made her feel that way, especially when half the time she was bound and determined to find fault with him. But this time, she pushed all of that aside.

Her sister was in trouble. And Alice didn't have anyone else to turn to. So while Jonah hurried her back into the kitchen, she silently asked God to protect Lorene and her baby.

Jonah squeezed her hand. "It's going to be all right, Alice."

Alice figured he couldn't know that for certain, but his words did bring her a bit of courage and a little peace.

Almost.

Chapter Seven

"Her blood pressure is high and there's a possibility the placenta could separate from the fetus."

Alice kept hearing the doctor's words over and over as she sat outside the emergency room of the regional hospital. Jay had driven Lorene the twenty miles in record time with Alice and Jonah right behind them.

"Thank you for coming," she said to Jonah now. It was late and he looked tired. His eyes were laced with smoky circles of fatigue and his dark hair was messy and wind-blown. He held a plastic cup half-full of cold coffee.

"Not a problem." He looked down the hall toward the double doors. "So…they're keeping her overnight?"

Alice nodded. "Her blood pressure needs to come down and they have to monitor the placenta. If she's better in a couple of days, she can go home. But she'll have to stay in bed for the rest of the pregnancy. That won't be easy for Lorene. She can't sit still for very long."

Jay came through the doors and headed toward them. "They're moving her to a private room in the maternity ward. She might have to stay in the hospital for the next few weeks. Of course, she's begging the doctor to let her go home and rest there, but I'm afraid something will happen to her and the baby if she's not near the hospital."

Alice nodded. "We'll make sure she gets her rest, Jay. Don't worry."

"How can I not worry?" her brother-in-law asked. "What if something goes wrong? What would I do, Alice?"

"We won't let anything happen to them," Alice answered. "You have me, and your parents said they'd help, remember?"

Jay nodded. "I'm sure glad they live nearby."

Alice hugged him close. "They love Lorene as much as you do. We'll all make sure she's okay. We have to pray that she'll be just fine."

Jay pulled back. "I'm going to stay here

for a while longer, just to make sure she's settled in. I might stay all night. I don't want to leave her."

"Want me to stay, too?" Alice asked.

"No, no. You go on home and check on the cats. You know the two she leaves food for out in the back garden?"

"I'll make sure the cats are fed," Alice said, her heart going out to Jay. He loved her sister so much.

"I can help, too," Jonah said, shrugging. "With whatever you need, I mean. Anything."

She glanced over at Jonah and read something there in his expression. Maybe he felt as she did—a bit envious but also very protective. The love between her sister and Jay was something to behold. Who wouldn't want that kind of devotion and unity? Alice prayed for the little baby they'd waited so long to have. *Please, Lord, keep them in Your heart. Help them.*

Jonah took her by the arm. "You look exhausted. Let's get you home."

"Maybe I should stay." She glanced around at Jay.

"Go on with Jonah, you hear? My mama's coming back. She just went to get my dad a pack of peanuts from the vending machine. She'll send him home soon and, knowing her, she'll stay right here with me."

"You'll call me if anything changes?"

Jay nodded. "You know I will."

She'd talked to Lorene earlier, but Alice wished she could see her again. "Will you tell her…that I love her?"

"I will," Jay said, grinning. "She knows that, but she'll want to hear it."

Alice turned to Jonah. "I guess I'm ready." Then she waved to Jay. "I'll come by first thing tomorrow to check on her, okay?"

"Okay." Jay sank down on one of the waiting room chairs, his head in his hands.

"I shouldn't leave him," she said to Jonah as he escorted her toward the lobby and the parking lot.

"I could stay with you," Jonah offered, stopping her just outside the doors.

The night was windy and chilly. Winter was coming soon. Alice wrapped her arms around her body, shivering.

And Jonah was there, offering her his jacket. "Here. It's getting colder."

She nodded. "I can't stop shivering."

He pulled her close. "Do you want to go back inside?"

"No," she said. "No need for you to stay, too, Jonah."

"I don't mind. Whatever you want to do."

She looked back, torn. "I should probably go home and check on those stray cats. Lorene will be as worried about them as she is about herself."

"Then we'll feed the cats and I won't leave until you feel okay."

She got into his pickup, wondering why she hadn't noticed his kind nature before. Maybe because she'd been too busy judging him?

"Thanks again for getting me to the hospital."

"I couldn't let you drive. You were as upset as Lorene and Jay."

"They've waited for this baby a long time," she replied, looking out the truck window. The streets were deserted this time of night. The whole world slumbered while the cold wind howled and danced all around them.

"They love each other."

His statement shocked Alice. She turned to stare over at him, a hundred questions popping into her head. "What about you?"

"What about me?" he asked, giving her a quick look.

"Tell me about your family, Jonah."

* * *

Jonah watched the dark road back toward Bayou Rosette. How could he tell her what he didn't really know? Should he tell her the truth—that he was raised in a children's home with twenty other boys until he'd been sent to a foster home and that he didn't actually have a family to call his own? Maybe he could just give her the general stuff without going into detail. But tonight…he needed to talk about it. Really talk about it. And the darkness gave him the courage to do it.

"I…uh… My foster mother passed away while I was in college."

He heard her intake of breath. "Foster mother?"

Jonah nodded. "Yes. I never knew my real mother. Or my real father. I lived in a children's home for a while and after that I always had Aunt Nancy—she was my foster mother. She was good to me."

"Good to you? Is that all you can say about her? Did you love her?"

"Why would you ask that?"

She was silent for a while then she said, "Well, because I…I want to know that you had a good life. I want to know you were happy. And there's a difference between someone just being good to you and truly loving you."

"I had a good life and I was content," he replied.

"But?"

"But—" He stopped, wondering how to word what he needed to say. "But…as good and kind as she was, she wasn't my flesh and blood. Don't get me wrong. I loved Aunt Nancy but I always wondered, you know? You're blessed to have people who love you, Alice. Lorene is blessed to have Jay and a baby on the way. They make a nice family."

"I am blessed," she said. "But I miss our parents every day. I can't imagine never knowing your parents, though. That must be awfully hard on you."

She'd never know just how hard. "I get by. And I learned a long time ago to rely on myself. That's how I manage. And I guess that's why I'm a loner. I got tired of living in that crowded orphanage. Now I like my privacy."

"And you don't appreciate people snooping in your business?"

"No, I don't. So from now on, if you want to know something, just ask me. I'll try to be honest with you."

She lowered her head. "Okay. I'm sorry I followed you today. It was wrong. But I have my own reasons for avoiding you, Jonah. It stems from being duped…by Ned. But I shouldn't take that out on you. It won't happen again. Besides, I need to get on the ball with this story for the magazine. What you're doing is important for our area. I'm sorry I've been such a pain."

"Let's drop it," he said, wishing he could tell her everything he had on his mind. "I just have a lot to deal with and…I'm not one for turning to others for help."

She shot him a confused glance. "What about your faith? What about God?"

"I don't rely on Him too much either. I don't think I'm on God's radar. I always let Aunt Nancy do the praying while I just got on with things." How could he explain that he'd always believed God had deserted him?

Alice didn't want to push him on his faith, so they were silent for the last few miles. He pulled the truck up to the house, then got out before Alice could protest.

"You don't have to escort me to the door," she said as he helped her out of the pickup.

She didn't know what else to say after his

admission about his past. But his honesty had done what all the snooping in the world couldn't do. It had endeared him to Alice and...made her see that she had rushed to judgment. Jonah obviously had his own reasons for coming to Bayou Rosette. Maybe he really did need to build these homes.

"Yes, I do," he replied. "I'm not leaving until I know you're all right. This place is kind of isolated."

Alice glanced around, seeing her beloved home in a new and different way. It *was* isolated here. She'd never been alone here that much. She'd always had family around.

His gallantry shouldn't make her feel good, but it did. Not that she was afraid to be alone. She wasn't. It was just that tonight of all nights, she didn't *want* to be alone. And she had a feeling Jonah needed to talk to someone, too. But she had to be sensible.

"You can't stay all night, Jonah."

"I know that, but I can stay until you're feeling better. Until Jay calls, which I'm sure he'll do soon."

"Okay, just for a while." She motioned toward her apartment. "I'll make some decaf. And I think I have some cookies Lorene made earlier in the week."

"That would be good."

Alice headed up the stairs, aware of his boots hitting the wood behind her. And she had to wonder if Jonah had come here to build more than just houses.

Maybe he was searching for a home, too.

"I like your apartment."

Alice turned to find Jonah staring at some primitive watercolors she'd bought in a shop in Natchitoches. "Thanks. I paid to have this wing of the house remodeled into an efficiency apartment and I decorated it myself."

"Judging from your eclectic décor, you seem to like the local traditions, same as me."

She placed freshly percolated coffee on the table then set down a plate of snickerdoodle cookies. "It's ready."

Jonah came and pulled out a chair. "Alice, I think I need to explain…about being at Arnold Gauthier's place."

Alice's heart bumped against her ribs. "I'm listening."

"It's nothing as sinister and underhanded as you might have imagined," he said, his eyes going soft. He reached for a cookie, then dropped it on the bright pink napkin she'd put on the table for him. "I mean, think about it. I've come here to build houses, new houses. But I want them to have an old feel about them. I want this new subdivision to blend in with the bayou and the countryside. So I've been reading up on the local history—all parts of it. I told you that article you wrote about Rosette House brought me here, but that's just the beginning."

Doubt nudged at Alice, making her want to lash out at him again. But he'd been kind and steady tonight when she'd been terrified for her sister, and he was trying to be honest with her now. She had to at least give him a chance. "I can buy that. It just struck me as odd that you'd go to all that trouble to find out more about the Mayeaux family." She twisted at her napkin. "And honestly, that whole feud thing is kind of lame. A lot of it happened before we were born, but we heard about it growing up. And our parents tried to be kind to them. They mostly just stole stuff and vandalized our property some. I think they were just poor and wanting food from our garden, which my mother would have gladly given them anyway. Did Mr. Gauthier tell you what you wanted to know?"

He took a long sip of coffee then gave her a direct look. "If you mean, did he tell me that the Mayeaux were more like a gang of outlaws than good, upstanding citizens, yes, he told me that. And he also told me that they sold their land rather abruptly many years ago and then they left. They have a very colorful history, apparently. I wonder what became of them."

She shrugged. "I've never heard much since they left. I guess that's why I was so surprised that you wanted to know more—they don't even live here now. But then, history is full of both good and bad characters, I reckon."

"Yes, and those characters, good and bad, have backgrounds and roots and family and...I like hearing all the details. I wanted details, so I went to the source by visiting Mr. Gauthier. Same as I did when I came here to see you."

She had to smile at that. "But I haven't been very cooperative, have I?"

"No, you haven't. Even Old Man Gauthier, shotgun and all, has been nicer than you about things around here."

"I can change that," she said, getting his raised-eyebrow look. "I can give you the tour of Rosette House, right now, tonight."

His eyes lit up. "Are you sure? I mean, it's kinda late."

"I can't sleep," she replied, finishing off her cookie. "I'll carry my cell with me in case Jay calls, but yes, I think now is a good time to go down memory lane. It'll take my mind off Lorene and the baby and reinforce why I believe in family so much." She took their cups to the sink, then turned to stare at him. "And…I want you to know that there is such a thing as family, Jonah. I'm sorry you never had that. Even the Mayeaux with all their antics were a family, from what I've heard. So…if you came here to find that, well, you're in the right place. And I'm willing to help you create the kind of homes that will make families safe and cozy. I won't fight you anymore."

He got up, his smile soft and sure. "I'd appreciate that." He let out a great breath. "You have no idea how relieved I am to hear that. Now, if you can just back off on the shadowing, just enough to give me some breathing room and…just watch me work, Alice. Watch and listen and observe, but please don't go digging behind my back, okay?"

Alice didn't know whether to laugh or to go back to doubting him. Was he being nice just to win her over, or did this man really have a soft spot for home and hearth?

Reminding herself that he'd gone through life without a family to call his own, she softened her doubts, hoping to meet him halfway. "I just have one more question for you," she said, determined to stop putting obstacles between the man and the work he seemed intent on doing here. "I just need to know once and for all why you chose Bayou Rosette. And you'd better be completely honest with me. I need that. I need you to be honest. I can accept that you were fascinated with my brilliant writing abilities and that you love history. But I think there's more to this. And I think you need someone to talk to about that, so I'm here and I'm listening."

He stood across from her, his eyes going dark with some unreadable emotion, a pulse throbbing in his jaw. "I should have known there was a catch."

"No catch. Just getting down to business, you know. Cutting to the chase. I like things simple and direct."

He nodded. "I think I can handle simple and direct, but…my reasons for coming here aren't that simple."

"I'm willing to listen to any and all explanations," she said. "I didn't ask questions with Ned. He just came in and caught all of us at a very bad time, when we needed someone to believe in. We all trusted him way too much and when he left…well, I wasn't the only one he hurt. So if I'm being hard on you, it's because I can't bear to watch the people I love suffering again. And I won't ever go through that kind of pain and humiliation again, either. So just level with me so we *can* get on with this, okay?"

He looked down at the floor, then blew a breath out. "You don't stop, do you?"

"I can't afford any more mistakes, Jonah. My sister gave up all her dreams to stay here with me. I came back here to make sure she's taken care of. And if things go wrong on this project—"

"That wouldn't be your fault, Alice. You can't take on all the troubles that cross Bayou Rosette."

"But I can try to do my job and protect this place. That's why I came back here."

"Is it? Or are you just trying to make amends for your sister's sacrifices?"

He had her there. She was always trying to make amends. "Maybe. But it's worth it to me. That's what family is all about."

"Oh, I know all about family," he said. Finally, his hands on his hips, he glanced up and looked straight into her eyes. "My biological mother was a Mayeaux and I managed to trace her back to Bayou Rosette. And Mr. Gauthier is pretty sure she was the younger sister of the infamous Mayeaux brothers. But that's about all he could tell me. How's that for direct?"

Alice had to grab the nearest chair. "Wow."

"Yeah, wow. When I read your article, it triggered something in me—I had to know the whole story. So I *did* come here to build houses, but while I'm here I'd really like to find out something about my roots, or more specifically my lack of roots. Why did she give me up? That's the big question."

Alice's heart turned to mush. She could see the torment in his eyes, could feel the remorse, the confusion he must be feeling. And the shame. "Jonah, I'm so sorry for all I said earlier and for spying on you. And…I'd be willing to help you answer that question, if you want."

"I don't want any pity or regret, Alice. And I don't expect you to understand this. You don't need to get involved. It's just something I need to work through myself. While I do my job."

"I'm not the pitying kind," she retorted.

"This is just me offering to help you with research—to get those answers you need. I'm good at digging in the past. And I'd like to know the truth, same as you. No strings attached. I'm just like you in that way. I like to stay busy. And since you've got a lot to do while you're here, I can help you. I want to help you—now that I understand."

He reached out a hand to her, his eyes full of defeat and defiance. "Why don't you show me the house and we'll talk about it."

"Fair enough." She grabbed her cell and the keys to the rest of the house. Wanting to lighten things, she said, "Oh, and I might add, in our own way, we're just about as colorful as the Mayeaux family. Just in case you were wondering."

"You, colorful?" He laughed out loud as he guided her down the steps toward the first level of the old house. "I would never have imagined that."

Alice chuckled, too, thinking his laughter was brittle and forced. But she wouldn't push him on the issue of his mother anymore tonight. She had to honor his request to back off. "I guess you've seen some of my colorfulness, huh?"

"Yes, I have. But I don't mind one bit. It's

part of what I like about you. And because I like you, I want you to understand that I came here with the best of intentions. I want to help rebuild your town, Alice. And your article, coupled with what I'd found out about my mother, started this whole path that brought me here. I'll admit I haven't been handling that very well, but that's the honest truth, plain and simple."

His words, spoken so low and so close, brought a warm shiver of awareness down Alice's spine. She'd have to watch herself with this one. She could easily fall sway to his charm and his goodness, but now that she knew some of his motivation for coming here, she could also help him out if he'd let her.

She glanced around, not afraid of the darkness, but afraid of this brilliant light of hope shining throughout her system. She couldn't turn toward that light. Not just yet.

Jonah might be kind and good and full of great intentions, but he could also prove to be dangerous, too. Dangerous for her bruised, battered heart.

Chapter Eight

The leaves were changing. Jonah sat at his favorite table at the Bayou Inn, scanning his e-mails on his laptop. Lorene was resting at home now with strict orders from her doctor to stay off her feet. Alice had been going back and forth from work to home over the last week to make sure Lorene followed orders. Jay was apparently doing the same, checking on his wife as often as possible when he wasn't at his family farm a few miles away.

And Jonah had not only survived the town hall meeting, but most of the good people of Bayou Rosette were supporting him one hundred percent on his plans for the subdivision. Next week, he'd start building the first model home just down from Rosette

House, but near the park he already had a team carving out for construction across the footbridge from Rosette House.

Rosette House was amazing. In spite of blurting out that night his need to find his biological mother, he'd enjoyed the tour of the beautiful old cottage. Alice's pride had shown through as she described each room and its contents with loving detail.

He'd enjoyed watching her talk, watching her walk, watching her laugh. Yep, things were sure different now. Alice had even invited him to church and he'd gone. The sense of community hadn't stopped at the church doors. This was a place of faith. Strong faith. And maybe he *did* need that element in his life right now.

And Alice… Alice was being so meek and mild he was beginning to wonder if she'd just tuned him out completely. Surely he hadn't won her over to the point that she no longer questioned his every move, had he? Maybe now that she knew about his possible parentage, she'd backed off, disgusted and revolted by his claim. And she'd been so preoccupied with her sister's pregnancy, maybe she'd put her doubts and concerns regarding him on hold. They had a couple of weeks left before she finished her piece on this project, but she had yet to actually comment or give him her true opinion on the plans he'd shared with her. Or about his mother.

Jonah hoped he wouldn't be blindsided by her words in the article. And he hoped she wasn't put off by the possibility of his being related to the Mayeaux family. He was supposed to meet her here, so he'd soon get a chance to question her, he hoped.

"Want more mint iced tea?" Paulette Germain asked as she tapped a finger on the table.

"I'm good, thanks," Jonah said, pushing up out of his thoughts. "Did you read the article in the paper today, about the subdivision?"

"Sure did," Paulette said, grinning, her brown eyes merry. "I think you're good to go, Jonah. I haven't seen this much excitement in this town since Paul Newman passed through making a movie. We needed this boost, that's for sure."

"I'm glad," Jonah said. "We've already started clearing land for the park and the first phase of houses. We break ground soon on the model home."

"We're all anxious to see the first house," Paulette said. "And we can't wait to read more about it in the *Bayou Buzz* magazine. Hear Alice is doing an in-depth article about it."

"She's working on it," Jonah said, wondering if Alice was actually working on the story.

"It'll sell a lot of copies, I'm sure," Paulette said as she saddled away, tea pitcher in hand.

Jonah smiled and nodded to a couple of the locals, thinking he liked the slow, easy routine of this tiny bayou town. No hurries, no rush, just good, solid people working each day to get to the next. Church on Sunday and renewed hope on Monday. He could get used to this kind of life.

Even if he did have about a hundred e-mails from his secretary back in Shreveport. They were setting up construction sites and coordinating where all the workers would stay while the houses were being built. The land would be cleared section by section, and he planned on using as many locals as he could for that and the construction. Thus the e-mails and phone calls. He had to make sure he brought in an expert team, but he also wanted to keep the locals heavily involved.

He glanced over the plans he had saved on the laptop, particularly the plans for the model home. He couldn't wait to get started on this home. It would be the centerpiece of the whole subdivision, a place that should draw people in and make them feel welcome. Which was why he wanted to know what Alice thought about it. Why hadn't she spoken to him about the plans? He'd changed them up since he'd shown her that first draft, based on what he'd seen after they'd toured Rosette House. He wanted the first home to look as if it had always been there—very new but with an old feel. Now he was anxious to show her the things he'd added, too. That is, if she showed up for their meeting.

"So, how's the story on Jonah going?"

Alice spun around in her chair to find Dotty standing behind her, tugging on one bright teal-colored hoop earring, her eyes as liquid as hot chocolate.

"It's going," Alice replied, closing the genealogy screen she'd been studying. "We've reached a kind of truce. The town meeting helped clarify some of the confusion and the town council gave Jonah the go-ahead, so he's going to proceed with his plans."

Dotty made a sound in her throat. "Yeah, I was there, remember? So, I get that. Could you possibly be a bit more forthcoming? I need details on the article you're writing."

Alice couldn't hedge much longer. "I've got lots of notes and I've studied the initial plans for this new community. The whole town is behind this, so I can't see any reason not to write a glowing article. It's good for the economy and Jonah's planning on hiring lots of locals to help with the whole process. It means jobs and it means action in this place and that's something we all need around here."

Dotty made that annoying sound again. "Speaking of action, how are things between you and the subject of this article?"

"What do you mean?"

"Now, honey, don't play coy with me," Dotty said, her fringed plaid shawl cascading off her shoulders. "I see how that man looks at you and I see how you watch him. There is sure some kind of spark between you two."

"I'm keeping things professional," Alice retorted. She didn't add the part about doing heavy research into Jonah's possible link to the Mayeaux. Nobody knew she was doing that, not even Lorene. Then she glanced at her watch. "And speaking of that, I'm supposed to meet him at the Bayou Inn, then drive out to the property this afternoon. He wants to show me where they'll break ground for the first house. I thought I'd get some pictures. The official ribbon-cutting and dirt-shoveling ceremony is scheduled for Friday, so I'll be there for that, too."

"Got it all worked out, I see," Dotty said, shaking her head. "I can't wait to read this piece."

"I'm getting it together," Alice replied, wishing that were true. She had yet to write one word. But she'd get there. If she could just figure out what was holding her back. Was she too close to the subject this time? Too close to be objective and fair? Or was she more preoccupied with finding out more about Esther Mayeaux?

"I've got to go," she told Dotty, deciding she couldn't worry about all of this right now. Then she shut down her laptop and grabbed her tote bag. "I'm late for a meeting with Jonah."

"Hold on."

Alice turned to find Dotty staring at her, her hand on her hip, her eyes squinting in that Dotty way that zoomed in like precision radar. "What is it?" Alice asked, fidgeting.

"That's what I'm trying to figure out," Dotty said through her squint. "You're usually so talkative about your stories. I mean, I have to tell you to be quiet and write the story, already. But this time, you've been as quiet as a mouse. Now, why is that? And how come you didn't ask one question at the town meeting?"

"Jonah had already answered most of my questions," Alice replied, shifting her feet against her wedge loafers. "I took a lot of notes."

"Really, now? How interesting."

"What's your point?" Alice asked, knowing Dotty liked to play with words before she finally got to the bottom of a situation.

"My point—things are somehow different with you these days. I'm worried. Are you losing your edge?"

Alice dropped her tote back on the desk. Leave it to Dotty to zoom right in on her own fears. "My sister is pregnant and on bed rest. Jay is working day and night and worrying about his wife, and I'm trying to take up the slack when he and his parents can't be there with Lorene. I haven't slept very well. And I'm trying to get a handle on this story and what Jonah's building this community will mean to this town. So give me a break, okay?"

Dotty chewed at her lip. "Okay, then. Just

checking. I was afraid you've gotten a tad too close to your subject on this one."

"Jonah and I have reached a turning point," Alice said, careful to avoid eye contact. If Dotty knew Jonah might be related to the Mayeaux family, she'd want the whole story and she'd want it in print. Alice couldn't do that to Jonah. This was his secret and his story to share with the world. Alice couldn't break the fragile trust she and Jonah had built up over the last few days. She wouldn't do that, even for a good story and even if her perceptive boss had picked up on it. "It's okay, Dotty. I'm going to put this story together well before the deadline."

"Well, see that you do. We've got a magazine to put out, after all."

"I'm aware of that." Alice got out the door before her boss could question her any further. Or before she began questioning herself again. When she walked into the Bayou Inn, she saw Jonah waiting at their favorite table, his smile tentative.

Alice liked his smile. So she smiled back. It didn't hurt to be nice to the subject matter, now did it? Besides, she'd done a lot of late-night research regarding his mother. Now she just had to decide if she should tell him or not.

* * *

Jonah dropped his pen then leaned forward. "So…are you ever going to tell me what you think? I mean, really think—about my house plans?"

Alice fussed with her cranberry muffin. "I wanted to wait until I could get the whole picture. I need to put it all down in words."

"So can you at least tell me anything, good or bad, about the model house?"

"It looks nice," she said. "I'd have to see the real house before I commented. I can't judge from the blueprints."

Jonah didn't like the sound of that. "I see. So I guess I have to wait right along with everyone else to read your article, right?"

"Right. We don't usually let our subjects have editorial control over what we print."

"I wasn't asking for editorial control. Just wanted a hint as to the slant of your story."

"The slant will be pro-community, trust me. I think I'd get run out of town on a rail if I voiced any protest against your new subdivision."

"I still have to give it a name, don't I?"

"Yes, you do. What's holding you back on that?"

He wanted to laugh at how she'd managed

to turn the tables on him. "I can't decide. It has to be right, you know."

"I get it. You want the name to reflect all you've put into this place, right?"

"Yeah, something like that."

She finished her coffee and muffin. "Let's go out there and have a look."

Surprised at this burst of enthusiasm, he dropped some cash on the table and waved good-day to Jimmy and Paulette. "We can take my truck," he said as they headed out the door.

"No, I'll follow you. I'll check in on Lorene before we get started, then probably just call it a day after this so I can sit with her awhile this afternoon. I can work from home and get a lot done."

"Okay. I'll see you out there, then."

A few minutes later he watched as she turned off to Rosette House. He turned after her and decided to park on that side of the bayou so they could walk over together. He waited for her to go in and check on her sister, then smiled at her when she came out the front door. "How is Lorene?" he asked, taking in the way her floral skirt flirted with her shapely legs.

"She's doing pretty well, considering she hates sitting still. I think she's knitted about six pairs of baby booties and two more blankets."

He smiled at that. "Your sister will be a good mother."

"Yeah, she's more maternal than I am."

They stopped in the middle of the footbridge. "You don't want children?" he asked, wondering why it mattered to him one way or the other. He certainly knew from personal experience that not every woman wanted to be a mother.

"Oh, sure, one day," she said.

She didn't sound so convincing. Jonah guided her on down the bridge, thinking they had a long way to go in the being-comfortable-around-each-other department. And yet, he wanted her to feel comfortable with him. And with this project.

"So," he said as they reached the clearing for the park, "you'll notice we're leaving the old magnolia trees and most of the cypress trees and pines. I want the park to look natural, as if it's always been here. I plan on planting some azaleas and crape myrtles, too. And maybe some dogwoods."

She glanced around, the crisp afternoon wind playing in her golden curls. "You left the old live oak. I'm so glad. I've climbed that tree more times than I can remember, usually when I was mad at my parents or Lorene."

"I'm sorry about your parents," he said, meaning it. "Your family sounds so close."

"We were close. They were good parents—strict at times and lenient at others, but always loving and consistent."

Jonah wondered what that was like, having real parents to guide you. "Aunt Nancy was the same. She was sweet and kind, but firm with those of us who passed through her doors."

"How long were you with her?"

"I got there when I was ten and I stayed through my teen years. I aged out of the system, so I had to move on. College came next and then work, lots of hard work, until I could get a loan to open my own construction firm. She died before I graduated."

"She'd be proud of you, I'm sure."

"I'd like to think so."

"The park looks promising," she said, her eyes downcast.

Was she hiding the pity he figured she felt for him?

"I'm glad you approve." He tugged at her arm. "Now, come on around the curve and I'll show you where the model house will be located."

She followed him, trudging through dried clay and clumps of grass and tire marks to another clearing. Then she let out a little squeal. "You can really see all of Rosette House from here. What a view."

Pleased as punch that she'd noticed that right off the bat, he said, "I planned it that way. From here the house takes your breath away, don't you think?"

She nodded. "Sometimes I forget just how beautiful my home is. And I've never seen it from this angle. It's a perfect view of the house and the gardens."

"Well, I saw it right away." He held back, wishing he could tell her the whole truth. All of it. But it was still too amazing and too painful to remember when he'd first seen this house. So he told her about the day he'd come here for the first time to see it in person. "I was out here walking…that day you saw me. And I stopped right here and turned and I knew this was the perfect spot to begin. A good spot to build something new and good, right here in the shadow of that pretty piece of property. Whoever lives here will be able to see your home every day."

"I wonder who that will be," she said, her voice dreamy. "Maybe a young couple with two toddlers? Or an older couple looking to retire in a small town."

Jonah swallowed the breath he'd been holding. She looked so content, so full of pride at that moment that he wanted to take her into his arms and hug her close. But he couldn't do that. And he couldn't tell her that he would probably be the one living here and seeing that view every day because he'd only now decided that.

He wanted to stay here, just so he could be near her, and so he could be in the place where he was pretty sure his mother had stood so many times in her life.

Chapter Nine

"Wow, it's getting late," Alice said about an hour later. "I should go check on Lorene again."

Jonah swatted at a horsefly. "I didn't mean to keep you out here in the woods all afternoon."

"It's okay. This will help more with my article than all the research I've done on my own."

"You've researched me? Even after I told you just to ask me?"

She frowned at the disapproval in his eyes. They'd made a lot of progress this afternoon. She didn't want to ruin that. "Well, yes. Just for the article. I wanted to know your background. Very impressive. First in your class at Louisiana Tech while you worked at construction sites to pay your way through school. I never doubted you were a workaholic, Jonah. I just doubted your reasons for being here."

"And now that you know I'm a poor orphan boy, you've softened toward me. I guess I should be grateful for the pity vote."

Alice didn't like his tone or the way he looked off in the distance instead of at her. "Hey, nobody's pitying anyone around here. I've had some hard knocks, too, but I'm a firm believer in getting on with things. Lorene reminds me on a daily basis to turn to God when I'm having a pity party. I suggest you do the same and thank Him for helping me to change my tune about you. I know I've certainly prayed to Him for that to happen."

"I'm sorry," he said as they reached the porch at Rosette House. "I guess I'm a little rattled about the whole orphan thing. Growing up, it wasn't easy trying to explain that. So I quit explaining. That rule has stayed with me, I'm afraid."

Her heart got all sympathetic but she didn't let those protective feelings show in her voice. "Well, I'd say you don't have to explain anything now. You've more than proved you're the real deal—and not just to me. The whole town is buzzing about this."

He actually laughed at that. "Oh, that is a change of tune, all right. You wanted me to explain *everything* before. I practically had to give you a statement signed in blood."

"But as you can see, I can be reasonable," she said as she motioned to two wrought-iron chairs and a matching table on the porch. "I wanted solid explanations and now that I have them, I understand. You came here to find your roots and, in the meantime, help rebuild this town in the only way you know how—through architecture and construction. I'd say that's putting your talents to good use."

He slanted his eyebrows at her. "And I'd say you almost sound as if you're starting to like me a little bit more."

Alice felt the warmth of his incredible eyes on her and tried not to squirm. "I like the way you talk about your subdivision. All that stuff about using natural products such as limestone, and recycled and old wood, and solar panels that look pretty and artsy instead of creepy, not to mention nontoxic paint. And I have to admit I would have never believed milk jugs and wood chips could be recycled into composite building materials or pretty picket fences. And who doesn't like the sound of rain falling on a metal roof? All great ideas for a green community."

"Now you're just making fun of me, aren't you?"

"No, I'm not," she said. "You know, you need to lighten up just a bit."

"About what?"

"When I first met you, I saw this confident, determined man who had a vision. But you seem unsure of yourself these days and I can't understand why. It's almost as if you feel inferior now that I know the truth about you." She sat up, her eyes catching his. "Jonah, I don't judge people in that way. I might not trust con artists, but I know now that you're not that kind of man. And if you're the least bit embarrassed by your past, you need to drop that notion right now. I don't think any less of you because of who your mother might have been."

She watched as he struggled to control his emotions. He seemed both amused and irritated. But there was something else there in his gray eyes, a dark longing that tugged at her heart. He let out a sigh. "I'm glad to hear that, but—"

"No buts. In fact, I've been doing some research on the Mayeaux myself. And I think I might have found something to help you."

"Really? Even after I asked you not to do that? You don't listen very well, do you? Researching me and my family, just like that."

"Yep, and before you get all angry and defensive about your privacy, just remember I'm trying to help. And if you give me a few minutes to go in and check on Lorene and see what I can heat up for supper, you can stay and help us eat whatever casserole the church ladies sent over today. And I'll be glad to talk to you about all of this after dinner. That is, if you want to stay."

She didn't give him a chance to answer. "I'll be right back."

Jonah watched as she pranced toward the wide front doors of the big house, wondering how he could tell her that being around her did make him nervous. Very nervous. He appreciated her need to help him, but he wasn't so sure he wanted Alice involved in the thick of things regarding his biological mother. Already, she'd gone behind his back again after he'd told her to let it alone. But that was just her nature, he reminded himself. Alice had a knack for getting to the heart of matters, for finding the truth. He should have remembered that before blurting out his past to her. And he'd have to be careful telling her anything else.

Too late now to change it. She wanted to help and he didn't know how to stop her. And maybe he didn't want to stop her, since it would mean he'd be able to spend more time with her.

Because he was beginning to care a lot about being around her all the time.

"I thought I heard someone talking to you."

Lorene's beaming smile belied the dark circles of fatigue underneath her eyes.

"Your ears are too big," Alice replied, pulling a big pan of chicken lasagna out of the refrigerator. "It's a business meeting, nothing more."

"And I guess inviting him to stay for potluck is a business decision?"

"Your imagination is also too big." Alice stuck out her tongue at her sister, then put the pan in the oven to heat up. "So I'll make a salad to go with this and we have brownies from Paulette for dessert."

"I could get used to this," Lorene said, her hand on her belly. "But I'm sure tired of sitting on my bottom doing nothing."

"You need to rest," Alice reminded her. "The nursery is ready and you have enough supplies to last until the kid starts college. I'd say you need to sit back and enjoy this quiet time."

"I guess you're right. Things won't be quiet around here when this little tyke comes along."

"I can't wait," Alice admitted as she came to sit across from the long floral couch where Lorene perched with her feet on a pillow. "I'm going to spoil the kid rotten."

"Are you gonna call him or her 'the kid' forever?"

"I'm just waiting on a name. And a little face to go with that name."

Lorene grew quiet and Alice glanced up to find tears in her sister's eyes. "What's wrong?"

"I'm okay," Lorene said, her voice shaky. "I just wish Mom and Dad could be here. I always thought they'd be right here, you know, to share their first grandchild. So many times, I've wished to hear Mamma's soothing voice, telling me it's gonna be okay."

Alice came over to the couch to hug her sister close, her own tears burning her eyes. "She is here, Lo. She's in every prayer, every wish, every touch. You know that, right?"

"Sure I do. I know God is listening and

Mom and Dad are right there with Him. It's so hard, sitting here worrying about what might go wrong."

"Nothing is going to go wrong," Alice assured her. "You just need to take care of yourself until the little fellow is ready to be born."

Lorene started giggling.

"What's so funny?" Alice asked, leaning away to stare at her sister.

"You, being the optimistic one," Lorene said as she wiped her eyes. "Now that's a switch for sure."

"I can be encouraging and upbeat, same as you," Alice retorted.

Lorene bobbed her head. "And I think I know why."

"Oh, and what do you think?"

"I think Jonah Sheridan has had a positive influence on you. I like seeing you smile and hum and act domestic. It's nice."

Alice shot off the couch. "I don't have visions of wedding cakes and bridal veils in my future, so don't even think that. Tried that once and it didn't exactly turn out the way I'd hoped."

"I didn't say you were dreaming of a

wedding, now did I? I just said it's good to see you happy for a change."

"Have I been *not* happy?"

"You've been bitter," Lorene said, her tone gentle.

"I think I had a right to be bitter."

"Yes, but it clouded your whole attitude. You didn't trust Jonah at first and now I think you do."

"I'm working on it," Alice admitted. "And if I don't get back out there, he's gonna think I forgot all about him."

"Go," Lorene said. "I'll holler when the oven buzzer goes off."

"Okay. You need anything? Want me to help you to the bathroom?"

"I'm fine. I had my quick bath earlier when Jay's mom was here and now I'm fresh as a daisy. A big, fat daisy."

"You're a cute daisy."

"Yeah, right." Lorene waved her away. "Go on. I'll be fine. I'll just catch up on the evening news while I wait for Jay to come home."

Alice headed back out toward the front porch only to find Jonah standing at the door. "Sorry. I was having a heart-to-heart with my sister."

"I heard," he said, his gaze moving over

her face in a way that made her heart speed up. "I mean, I wasn't deliberately listening. I just got up to come in and see if you needed any help and…I saw you two hugging and crying. I'm sorry."

"It's okay," she said, thinking it should bother her that he'd seen her being so open. But it didn't. Maybe because she figured he'd had a rough deal and he understood all about hiding your worst pain. "She's just all hormonal and worried. And…we both miss our parents."

He did something then that both surprised and troubled her. He put a hand to her face and wiped away a tear. "I understand," he said. "You know I understand."

And then he dropped his hand and kept looking at her, his eyes soft with longing and…wonder. "Now, what can I do to help with dinner?"

Now Alice was the one who was nervous. She had used her doubts and her bitterness like a sturdy shield, so she wasn't quite acclimated to Jonah's kindness. And yet, she thought as she watched him putting away dinner dishes, it had been right there all the time. He'd never been anything but kind to her, even when she was being such a brat toward him. She didn't deserve his kindness, but it sure worked as a balm on her bruised heart.

Better watch out for that, she cautioned herself. Don't get too comfortable. He might be kind and full of integrity but you can't fall for him. Too risky and too soon.

"Okay, I've waited long enough. So, what did you find out about my mother?"

Jonah's words in her ear caused Alice to glance up at him. "Let's go up to my apartment and I'll show you."

He nodded, his brow furrowed. "I'm still not so sure I like you doing research on my personal life, but I'm willing to listen to what you found."

Alice refrained from commenting, wondering why it should bother him that she'd decided to help him. Maybe he was still embarrassed by his past, or maybe he still had a few things he wanted to keep in the past. After giving Lorene a good-night hug and making sure she was comfortable, Alice told Jay they were leaving.

"Thanks for everything," Jay said, his eyes on his wife. "It means a lot to her that y'all spent some time with us tonight."

"You know I'll be here every night," Alice replied.

She and Jonah walked back up to her apartment. When she opened the door, she felt his hand on her arm.

"What?" she asked, turning to find his eyes on her.

"I envy that," he said, his tone low. "What's it like to have people around who love you?"

His question caught her off guard. "I'm not sure how to answer that. I've always been close to Lorene, even when we fought as teenagers about who'd get in the bathroom first. That's just the way our parents raised us."

He went to one of the big windows to stare out toward the bayou. "Before you tell me what you found out about my mother, I need to tell you something."

Alice's heartbeat hit full throttle. She didn't like the defeated tone in his voice and she dreaded hearing another unexpected admission. How could she trust him if he wasn't being completely honest with her? But she was willing to listen. "Okay."

He didn't turn around. "The first time I saw Rosette House was when I arrived at the children's home upstate." His shoulders slumped as he placed his hands in his pockets. "I don't know who dropped me off there—I was so young and so scared—but I do remember the old suitcase that came with me. Inside that suitcase was everything I had—some clothes, a pair of shoes and…a sketch."

Alice came to stand by him. "A sketch? You mean, some sort of picture?"

He nodded, swallowed. "Yes. It was a picture done in pen and ink—a sketch of Rosette House."

She turned toward him then, her eyes holding his. "Jonah? Are you sure?"

"Oh, yeah. I should know. The home director let me hang that sketch by my cot. I saw Rosette House every day, first thing in the morning and last thing at night. For a long time, I believed that was where I'd lived… before I was abandoned." He finally turned away from the window, a hand slicing through his dark hair. "Then when I realized no one was ever coming to get me, I figured living in such a house was just some sort of cruel dream. I'd never lived there. But someone must have, my mother maybe?" He laughed then, the sound like rattling ice. "But we both know that wasn't possible, don't we?"

Alice shook her head. "No. Only Brysons have lived in Rosette House. Maybe your mother bought the sketch at a local store or something?"

He leaned against the wall, his eyes going soft as he stared at her. "No, she didn't buy it, Alice. She drew it. It has her initials etched on it—hidden in one of the trees. My mother *did* live across the bayou, probably in some old shack or maybe a houseboat, but she lived here. I know that now from talking to Mr. Gauthier. He barely remembered her at first, but the more we talked, the more he did remember about a younger sister who left when she was a teenager. He said he didn't remember much about her, just the two brothers, and they and the father moved away shortly after the girl left. But I'm pretty sure she grew up here because I have that sketch as proof that she was here once. And I think she was an artist. Or at least she wanted to be an artist."

"So he couldn't be sure?"

"No." His smile was grim. "I keep wondering why no one can tell me anything more. I think something happened to her. Something so horrible that even old Mr. Gauthier didn't know about it. He thought it was a shame that no one knew much about the younger sister. It's as if my poor mother's existence has been wiped away."

He shrugged, then gave her a direct look. "So you said you might have some information on her? I'm almost afraid to hear it, but what did you find out?"

Alice didn't have a whole lot to tell him, but what she had might bring him some comfort. "Will you show me the sketch?" she asked.

"Sure. But first tell me what you know."

"I will," she said. "Oh, and, Jonah, how'd you get the last name Sheridan? Did you ever know your dad?"

Chapter Ten

Jonah wondered when he'd decided to open up his entire ugly past to this woman. He'd never talked to anyone but Aunt Nancy about these things and, even with her, he'd mostly listened while she'd tried to reassure him. He'd always held back and held on until the time when he'd be financially able to search for answers. So why was he putting himself through this with Alice? Maybe because he needed to talk to someone and, now that he was here where his mother had lived and he'd gone digging too deeply into the past, that need had increased. Or maybe because Alice made it so easy for him to relax and...trust. Alice was willing to fight for him, even if he wasn't so sure he wanted her to do that. He'd never depended on anyone else for help.

While it felt good it also felt alien. He still wasn't sure about all of this.

"That was the name I had when I arrived at the orphanage," he said, thinking he had nothing to lose at this point by answering her question. Any problems between Alice and him now were strictly personal. He could still get his work done, but he so wanted her approval—not just of his work, but of him as a person.

"You were given that name from birth?"

"As far as we know. I arrived at the orphanage without an official birth certificate—sure made things hard applying for jobs and such. Aunt Nancy helped me get a certificate even though we didn't have much information. No father was named, so I have no idea who my father was. But that's when I found out my mother's name, at least. We figured that's the name my mother wanted me to have—and that maybe my father was a Sheridan—and we never found evidence to dispute it or prove it."

"But you've never researched that name?"

He shook his head. "Look, whoever my father was, he left my mother high and dry. She didn't name him for a reason. I left it at that. I just want to find her—to ask her why she abandoned me. I don't care about my father."

Alice sank down at the dining table, then motioned to him to do the same. "Do you want anything to drink?"

"No. Let's just get on with this."

"When do you celebrate your birthday?" she asked, her expression blank in spite of the tiny pulse he could see near her temple.

"November," he replied with a shrug. "I was born in November—that much we know. Then, when I was around five, I came to the children's home the week of Thanksgiving. Abandoned at Thanksgiving. That kind of stuck, even after I was placed with Aunt Nancy. So she started celebrating my birthday every year during the week of Thanksgiving because she always told me how thankful she was to have me in her home and how I was a gift from God. A gift of wonder, she used to say, because of all the possibilities I had ahead of me."

"She sounds like a wonderful woman," Alice said, her smile warm and reassuring. "And I think she was right about you. You are full of possibilities. I'm just sorry I didn't see that right away."

Jonah didn't know how to react to her words. He was used to their sparring and banter, but completely unprepared for Alice's sweet and kind side. But, as usual, she was direct. It floored him. "I don't know about that. I just know I love my job as a developer and I love seeing new buildings go up. It's silly, but building homes and businesses makes me think of families. Happy families. And then I feel a part of something bigger than myself."

And he didn't have to get too close, building houses. He could observe what a true family was like without investing too much of himself in the outcome. He needed to remember that rule and apply it here in Bayou Rosette, too.

"That's not silly," Alice said. "That means you have a passion for your work. A lot of people go through life never feeling that way."

He lowered his head, uncomfortable with the praise. "So, what did you find?"

As if sensing they were treading on dangerous territory, Alice nodded and leaned close. "Well, I know a lot of people around here and I did some asking—very discreetly—and using the same excuse you gave me. I wanted to know more about the history of this area aside from Rosette House—for the article. People love to talk about the past."

"And?"

"And, I went back to Betty Nell and told her I was helping you with some of the historical information you'd been working on. When the Mayeaux clan came up, I asked about the sister again. Betty Nell told me what she could remember about Esther Mayeaux. She said Esther was a shy, quiet girl who stayed in the background. Her older brothers were notorious for making trouble, but Esther mostly went to school and did chores around the house. Their mother died when Esther was young, so it was kind of up to her to run the household while the brothers and the father worked the shrimp boats and did odd jobs to make money. Those three apparently drank away most of what little money they did make. And when they drank, things sometimes got ugly. But then, Mr. Gauthier told you they were kind of wild."

"Why didn't Betty Nell mention this to me when I was in the library the other day?"

"Because Betty Nell's not one for gossip, even if it is historical gossip. And probably because she wasn't so sure about you. She knows me and she loves to help me with research for my articles, even if most of this was off the record. But I am surprised Mr. Gauthier didn't tell you more."

"Maybe he didn't have a lot to say about Esther because she stayed hidden in the background." Jonah tried to imagine a petite, shy woman being bullied by her brothers and father. "That doesn't sound like a very good life, does it?"

"No. Betty Nell did remember how Esther would sneak into the library and read books on Saturday afternoons. And Betty Nell said if memory served her correctly, Esther actually won an art contest in high school."

Jonah noticed the way Alice's eyes lit up with this information. And for the first time in a very long time, he felt a sense of hope. "Really?"

"Yes, really. So I went through all the archives for the local paper—the *Rosette Gazette*. And guess what I found?"

Jonah didn't want to guess. He only wanted to see. "A picture of my mother, maybe?"

"Yes!" She got up and spun around, her excitement making her cheeks blush a pretty pink. After shuffling through some papers, she produced a copy of a grainy newspaper image. "Here it is."

Jonah stood up, taking the paper in his hands. It was an old picture and not very sharp, but he could just make out the tiny girl with the long brown hair. She was wearing a light-colored bow over her thick bangs. And she was holding a sketch, a soft, proud smile on her face.

Alice leaned over his shoulder. "I was so excited about seeing *her* I didn't pay much attention to the sketch." She looked down at the paper Jonah was holding, then quickly grabbed it away. "Jonah, look."

Jonah stared down at where her finger touched the picture near the sketch. "It's Rosette House," he said, his hand touching Alice's finger as he made sure. "It is, isn't it?"

"I think so," she said, her voice going soft. "You can see it better in this light. I never even connected on it."

"This is my mother holding a sketch of Rosette House," he said, the words confirming what they both could see. "I wonder if it's the same sketch I have."

"Where is that sketch?" Alice asked, so near he could smell the sweet scent of her perfume.

"It's in my room at the Bayou Inn. I had it framed long ago. I don't always carry it with me, but I especially wanted it here—for inspiration, I guess."

"I'd like to see it," she said, taking the

picture from him. "All evening I wanted to tell you about finding this clipping, but I wanted it to be just us when I did. I know how personal this is for you." She looked back at the grainy copy. "And now this—seeing the sketch makes it so real."

Jonah nodded and reached for her hand. Although he still wasn't so sure he wanted help in this, he was glad for this connection with his mother. "Thank you, Alice. I wanted to dig for this kind of information, but I've been so busy—and I have to admit I kind of dreaded finding the truth even though it's been a goal of mine most of my life."

"I don't mind helping," she said. "It's interesting and I'd want to know. I understand why you have to find your mother."

Jonah watched her face and saw the sincerity in her pretty eyes. And then he did something he'd never expected to do. He pulled her close, his eyes holding hers, and then he leaned down and kissed her.

Alice's heart skidded as she tried to find her equilibrium. She should have pulled back, but she couldn't bring herself to let go. Kissing Jonah seemed to make up for all the bad spots she'd had in the last few years—her parents' death, Ned's deception and her own heart's yearnings. How could she let go? But how could she hold on to such a wonderful hope, too?

So she stood back to stare up at him. "I…uh…"

"I know," he said, taking a deep breath. "I shouldn't have done that. You're not ready for this and I'm probably not, either."

"No, I didn't mean that," she replied, surprising both of them. "I mean, no, we probably shouldn't have kissed each other but I didn't mind that we did."

"Really?" He smiled then, a real smile that caused her to inhale a deep breath. "I didn't mind, either. It was…nice."

She bobbed her head. "So, we've established that kissing is good even though we probably shouldn't do it again."

"I think we've established that, yes."

They stood still for a few seconds, then moved toward each other, meeting halfway, their lips touching with a tentative kind of awe. "We should stop," he whispered, his lips touching hers. "We should…"

"Definitely." She pulled him close so she could enjoy the strength of his arms around her. "It's too soon."

A couple of minutes and another kiss later, he held her at arm's length again, his expression shuttered and unsure. "Okay, I'd better go."

She pushed at her curls, her gaze moving around the room. "Yes, you should."

She followed him to the door, then shoved the copy of the old newspaper page into his hand. "Take this."

"Oh, right. See how much you distract me?" But he said it with a warm smile. "Thanks again…for your help."

"You're welcome."

He tugged her back, kissing her one last time. "Good night, Alice."

She smiled at the husky tone of his voice. "Good night. I'll see you tomorrow, okay?"

"Yes, tomorrow."

After he left, Alice stared out into the moonlight, thinking that the word *tomorrow* had never held so many possibilities. And then she hit herself on the forehead. "What were you thinking, Alice Bryson?"

She hadn't been thinking. And for once, not thinking about things too much had felt really good. And so right.

But that didn't *make* it right. She knew that. And although her growing feelings for

Jonah were certainly different from the impulsive love she'd felt for Ned, things could still turn out the same. Jonah might walk away, too, because the realization of his mother's life here might be too much to bear. Alice needed to remember that. She couldn't force him to stay in a place that only reminded him of all he'd lost, could she?

So she turned out the lights and headed to bed, thinking she'd almost caved in to her feelings tonight.

Almost. Would she ever be able to let go and really live again? she wondered as she asked God for guidance and strength.

Jonah had never been one for turning to God a lot, even though Aunt Nancy had always encouraged him to do so. But tonight, as he stood on the bayou looking south toward Rosette House, he needed the Lord's comfort. He was so close to finding out the secret of his birth. Why had his mother left him so long ago? What had happened to that smiling young girl to make her just disappear? And now Alice had him wondering about his name and his father, too. He didn't want to know his father, had purposely put the man out of his mind. But that seed of curiosity had always been right there. Should he try to find out about that, too?

"Help me find the truth, Lord," he said into the night, wishing he knew how to pray. His scattered thoughts didn't seem to matter on this crisp fall night. The water moved in a steady, timeless rhythm toward the Mississippi River. The wind swirled and lifted in a pattern that only showed the changing of the seasons.

Jonah had never liked change, maybe because of the confusing ones he'd had to endure in his life, those jolts that had taken him out of time and place and left him alone and wondering. He wanted to settle in one spot, with the only changes those of the weather and good things happening. He built houses to bring about positive change and to help people find homes. He built houses because he'd always longed for a real home. And now he felt a big change coming, but this one wasn't out there in the world he tried to control and hold at bay. It was inside, in his heart.

Because of Alice.

He was falling for her and he'd tried to deny that. But tonight, holding her in his arms and kissing her had broken all the barriers he'd tried to put between them. This wasn't about building houses or putting a good spin on a story. This was about building a relationship with a woman who could make all of his dreams come true.

If he could get through to the real Alice. He knew she was hiding behind her scars and her wounds. He knew she still didn't completely trust him. But he wanted her to, so much. He wanted to see a change in her—a change of heart, so he could enjoy these feelings coursing inside him with the same swift current as the bayou's waters.

Because now, tonight, he finally understood what Aunt Nancy had tried to show him all those years ago. He saw that some gifts truly were wondrous and amazing. The gift of falling in love should be a cherished thing, a fragile, shining, cherished thing. Not something to be taken lightly. Not something he'd regret. For so long now, he'd fought against getting close to anyone. He'd fought against the need to find out the truth about himself, even when the need burned through him with every breath. And he'd held his secrets deeply locked inside his heart, guarding them with pride and humiliation. Maybe it was time to let go of all his shame and let both God and Alice into his life.

Could he do that? Did he dare let Alice continue searching for the truth about him?

He was ready for some sort of change, even if it did scare him with its intensity.

"How do I win her over, Lord? How do I make her see?"

And how did he find the courage to let her in?

Jonah had no answers, and maybe for now that would have to do. Maybe he'd just have to do as he'd always done and rely on himself to make things happen.

He clutched the copy of his mother's newspaper picture in his hand as he made his way toward his room. And he wondered again what had happened to her.

"Where are you?" he asked the wind. "And…where is my father?"

The wind lifted, rustling the paper against his hand.

God, the Father, is with you, he thought. That is a constant.

And that thought did bring Jonah a sense of peace, at least. But he knew that could be short-lived, too. So he didn't hold out much hope for his dreams. Or for Alice's change of heart, either.

Because sometimes, things changed for the worse, not for the better.

Chapter Eleven

"I'm waiting on that story."

Alice clicked her pen while she stared up at Dotty and wondered what to tell her boss. "I'm almost done."

"Almost don't cut it around here, suga'."

Alice gritted her teeth. She sure knew that, didn't she? And that sense of *almost* was what had her all in a tizzy. "I'll have it in a couple of days, I promise."

Dotty slid down in the chair next to Alice's desk, her brown silk tunic rustling over her winter-white knit pants. "You're acting weird, you know that? I think you have a thing for Jonah."

"How can you even say that?" Alice said, shuffling papers to avoid eye contact with Dotty.

But Dotty's jeweled fingers on her arm stopped her. "Look at me, Alice Bryson."

Alice glanced up, giving Dotty her best blank expression. "What?"

"Don't 'what' me," Dotty replied. She grabbed a piece of wrapped dark chocolate off Alice's desk, unpeeled the paper and popped the candy in her mouth. After she'd savored the chocolate, she said, "I've seen this before, remember? You got all quiet like this when you got involved with Ned Jackson. You get quiet and you get confused. And a confused reporter does not make for a good, solid story. Do I need to hold your hand on this one?"

Alice groaned, then dropped her head into her hands. "I did get that way with Ned, didn't I?" Glancing up through two fingers, she said, "Dotty, I think it's happening again. I…I really like Jonah. And it is like with Ned, but this time, it's different, too."

"Different, how?"

"He's *not* Ned. I can see that. He's really a nice man and he's not hiding anything illegal. He talks to me. This is not as fast and furious as what happened with Ned and I think that's good. It's kind of slow and steady and… special. Jonah is willing to let me in. I mean, he does now that—" She stopped, popping a hand over her mouth. "Never mind."

Dotty sat straight up. Alice wondered if the woman had an antenna on her head. "Go on. Now that...?"

"I can't explain. Jonah and I have had some personal talks, off the record. It's not for public scrutiny."

"Uh-huh." Dotty got up then leaned down. "I need an article, Alice, and soon. I don't mind one bit that you and Jonah are getting to know each other. I like the man and I think he's kinda cute. But...you've never been one to let anything get in the way of a good story. I'm just concerned that you're holding back on this piece for personal reasons."

"I told you, I'm fine. I've started the article and it'll be ready by Friday's deadline. Maybe it's different this time because I wasn't doing an article on Ned. I just fell for him and that was not work related, although I wish I had investigated him before I let him put that ring on my finger. But with Jonah, it was professional curiosity that made me go after him. Now our relationship is changing into something else. I've never had to deal with the two merging before, but with Jonah,

I have to be careful. I want the article to be fair but I don't want to hurt him, either."

"Wouldn't getting to the truth be better than worrying about Jonah's feelings?"

"He can take the truth and the truth is he's doing a good thing here. I didn't believe that at first, but now I do. I just don't want him to think I'm judging him, but I don't want the article to sound as if I've turned into an old softy, either."

"You're not making sense," Dotty said. She toyed with the pendant watch she wore on a long gold chain. "Time's a-ticking, honey. Get the job done, then you can enjoy your time with Jonah all the more."

"Good idea."

Alice watched as Dotty went on to torment the receptionist with questions about a supply order that hadn't come in. Good. Maybe she'd leave Alice alone for the rest of the day, at least.

Alice couldn't tell Dotty that she'd been splitting her time between the final edits on the article and doing research about the name Sheridan. And she didn't know how to tell Jonah what she had found so far.

It didn't look good. Not for him or the woman who had given birth to him. While no Sheridans had lived in Bayou Rosette, there had been a Sheridan in a town a few miles up the road. Alice had stumbled on this while doing a regional search. Could this Sheridan be related to Jonah's dad?

She didn't know. She only had a name and an address. Should she tell Jonah? Or should she stay out of it? She had promised Jonah she wouldn't go behind his back, but he hadn't gotten angry with her for finding the picture of his mother. Maybe he could handle this, too.

But first, she could just ride over and see for herself. That way, Jonah wouldn't have to know if this lead didn't pan out. What could that hurt?

She grabbed her tote, turned off her computer and headed for the door, calling to the busy receptionist.

"I'm off to do some legwork."

The girl behind the desk waved a hand to her, then went back to her typing. And Dotty was nowhere to be seen, thankfully.

Jonah watched as the construction crew worked on the park. He inhaled the smell of freshly turned dirt and grass mingling with the decay of the swamp and the last of the summer and fall blossoms. The park was taking shape, at least. The ground had been cleared and new grass was growing around the winding stone paths leading to the bayou bridge. He planned to rebuild the old bridge, keeping it the same but with new materials that would last a lot longer than the weathered, splintered wood holding it together now. Maybe he'd use stone there, too, and some sturdy cypress boards.

His construction foreman, Burt Holland, came up to him. "Hey, Jonah. You wanted to see me?"

"Yeah, Burt. Just wanted to check in. The park looks great. When will you be able to get back to the model house?"

"Probably tomorrow morning," Burt said, wiping the sweat from his leathery brow. "I know you want a rush on that one, boss, but we have to do things right or we'll get shut down."

"Yes, I want it right. We go by the book, no shortcuts. Just work as efficiently as you can. This house will be the showcase to draw buyers in."

"Got it. You can count on the crew. You know that."

"I sure do. And if this keeps up, I'll be putting you in charge of a lot more around here."

"I could use a pay raise," Burt said, grinning as he extended his hand.

"You'll get one, don't worry."

Jonah shook Burt's hand, and when the men left, Jonah turned to where the foundation for the model house had already been laid. The square slab of cement looked solid.

"A good foundation," he said to himself. Then he remembered something Aunt Nancy had told him once about the parable of the sower. Jesus had explained that some seeds fell on good ground and yielded a good crop, while others went into stony ground or fell by the wayside and produced nothing. He hoped the seeds he'd planted here would produce a vibrant new community.

I want this to be a solid foundation, Jonah thought. *I want that in my heart, Lord.*

Standing there, seeing that solid concrete simmering in the early-morning air, Jonah felt a sense of understanding at last. Aunt Nancy had always encouraged him to turn to God in all things. But he'd never actually forgiven God for seeming to turn away from him. He had blamed God, thinking both his mother and God had abandoned him. Why had he never asked God to show him the reasoning behind his life? And why had he never considered that God was his one true Father?

Maybe all of that early suffering brought me to this point, he thought. *Maybe I was meant to be standing right here, today.*

When he started connecting the dots and comparing the odd coincidences of his winding up here, he had to believe a higher power had helped in the planning. He wondered if building this new community would turn out to be worth all his angst.

Then he looked toward Rosette House and knew the answer. All of this had brought him to Alice. And she was worth his angst. But only if they could get past their hang-ups and get on with discovering each other.

That would become their foundation—learning to deal with past hurts so they could have a strong future. Wasn't that what love and forgiveness were all about? Could Alice forgive her con artist bridegroom enough to see that Jonah wasn't that way? And could he open up to her enough to show her everything inside his soul, good and bad?

"Penny for your thoughts."

He looked around to find Jay Hobert grinning at him.

"Hey there," Jonah said. "I guess I *was* lost in thought, huh?"

Jay looked bashful and nodded. "I get that way myself sometimes."

"What brings you by?" Jonah asked, glad for the company.

"Oh, I saw y'all over here and thought I'd take a sneak peek at all the action going on around here."

"Are we bothering Lorene? If we are, I can talk to the men."

"No, no. She's as excited as anybody about seeing things happening on the bayou. She never complains. Besides, she sits at the window and watches. Helps to keep her mind off worrying about the baby."

"Good. I know she needs her rest, but we have to stay on track. It gets noisy with all the big machines."

Jay chuckled. "She's married to a farmer, remember. Even though I keep most of my equipment over on my daddy's land, sometimes I bring a mower or a tractor home to use around here. She's used to loud engines and hammering."

"I guess so." Jonah wondered how Lorene and Jay made things work. "How long you two been married?"

"Five years," Jay offered. "But I've loved her most of my life."

"Really? How'd you know she was the one?"

Jay grinned, then looked across the water at his home. "When she smiled at me in high school, I just knew."

"And just like that, you two were together."

His hoot of laughter threw Jonah. "No. It wasn't that easy, now. Lorene had these big dreams about living in New Orleans and becoming an interior designer. But…she gave all of that up after her parents were killed in a car wreck."

Jonah nodded. "Alice told me a little bit about that. It must have been hard on them."

"It was. Lorene gave up college to stay here with Alice. By the time Alice was out of high school, Lorene and I were getting married. So Alice went on to college, but Lorene never did. She gave it up a second time to become my wife. That's why I try to make her happy every day of my life." He glanced up, his face turning red. "Sorry. I don't usually go on like that."

"No, I'm glad you did. I mean, I can tell you two belong together."

"I believe that," Jay said. "What about you? Ever been in love?"

Jonah didn't know how to answer that. "No, not really. I was always too busy planning my life."

"Better be careful there," Jay said. "Some gal might sneak up on you and change your ways."

Jonah looked toward Rosette House. "You mean some gal like Alice?"

"She's a sneaky one, all right," Jay replied as he turned to eye the foundation. "Can drive you crazy, but somehow she's lovable all the same."

"I hear that," Jonah said. "And I'll consider myself forewarned."

Jay walked the perimeter of the foundation. "This looks to be a nice-size house."

"It'll be spacious and cozy," Jonah replied. "It's sort of a replica of Rosette House. A smaller version."

"Interesting."

Jonah wasn't sure how to take that reaction. "What do you think about me being here, building this subdivision?"

Jay shook his head. "Me, I just want to be able to keep the land that's been in my family for several generations. I have no squabble with progress. We could use some new life on this bayou, that's for sure."

Jonah laughed. “Is that your way of staying out of things?”

Jay nodded, then tossed up a hand as he started back toward Rosette House. “You got that. I’ve learned that lesson well living with the Bryson sisters. You might keep that in mind, my friend.”

“I will,” Jonah said, wondering why Jay had made it a point to come over for a man-to-man talk. Was he trying to give Jonah some subtle advice?

Jonah figured he could use all the advice he could get. He was a stranger in a strange land, searching for a mother who would always be a stranger to him, wondering about his absent father and falling for the pretty, aggravating descendant of a local legend. When did he get so brave?

“Maybe not so brave, but very foolish,” he said to himself. “We’ll see soon enough.”

She probably shouldn’t be doing this, Alice told herself as she stepped up onto the old porch. But she had to know. For Jonah’s sake. Did the man who lived here know anything about Jonah? Did she even have the right Sheridan?

It was too late to worry about all of that.

She'd just get this over with and go home to visit with her sister and, maybe, see Jonah later.

She squinted toward the peeling house number, making sure she had the right address. Yes, this was definitely the place. Someone named Sheridan was supposed to be living here. But all she had to go on was S. Sheridan. Well, she'd sniffed out sources on less information. And since she'd driven the thirty miles to get here, she wasn't turning around now.

She was glad she hadn't told Jonah what she was doing this morning. She'd called him, promising to meet him later to go over the last few questions for the article. She wanted to interview him one more time, to put the finishing touches on her story.

Telling herself she'd only disappoint him if she was wrong about this person, Alice tentatively knocked on the rusted screen door. Listening, she heard a television blaring out the morning news and a dog barking somewhere inside the white wood-framed house. At least someone was in there.

And then the door creaked open and Alice was so shocked, she had to take a step back. She knew this man. He'd been the sheriff of the neighboring parish for years and he'd retired a while back. But his name wasn't Sheridan. It was Guidry. Samuel Guidry.

"Can I help you, young lady?" the old man asked, his eyes shining with agitation.

"I hope so," Alice replied. "Can I ask you a few questions?"

"Questions? What kind of questions?"

"About Esther Mayeaux," Alice replied.

The man shut the door in her face.

Chapter Twelve

Alice stood flabbergasted, then knocked again, determination overcoming her shock. "Mr. Guidry, please, I need to talk to you. It's important."

The dog's bark was louder this time. Maybe because the dog was now right behind the door. She stood back to listen again. The door didn't open. So she tried knocking one more time. "Mr. Guidry?"

"What do you want?" she heard over the dog's snarling barks.

"I need to find out if you know a woman by the name of Esther Mayeaux. It's really important."

"I don't want to talk about that."

"I really need to find out some information."

"Who are you?"

Alice hesitated, then decided to be truthful. "I'm Alice Bryson. I live down in Bayou Rosette. I work for a monthly magazine. I'm doing background research on a possible story. But I need to talk to you first."

She heard some rustling and then, thankfully, the dog's barks receded toward the back of the house. A door slammed and then she heard footsteps stomping toward the front door. The door creaked open, giving her a chance to see through the old screen.

"Hello," she said, letting out the breath she'd been holding. "I won't keep you long."

"I'm not talking to you. I've had my fill of reporters and people snooping around here."

What did that mean? "Recently?" she asked. "You've talked to someone else?"

"Not in a long time, no." The man stared her down as if she were one of the criminals he'd arrested in his time serving as sheriff. "I don't know anything much about that Mayeaux girl, haven't seen her in years. She was a liar, that's what she was. It's over and I'm not starting it back up. That girl was trouble."

Was? Alice didn't like the sound of that. "What do you mean? What happened?"

"You tell me," he retorted, his hand on the

door. "Sonny didn't do what they said he did, and if you're here because that kind of trash talk has been stirred up after all these years, well, you can just turn around and leave. And you'd better not print a word, you hear me?"

Sonny? S. Sheridan? She had to keep him talking. "Do you know Sonny?"

Finally, he let out a winded, cackling cough, then opened the door and came out onto the porch. Motioning Alice toward an old bench, he glanced around and, satisfied that they were alone, sank down in a nearby rocking chair. His frown only deepened the craggy crevices of his aged face. "Sit down, girl, and tell me why you're really here. I don't believe this is for a story—there ain't no story. At least there better not be. And you'd better not try any tricks. I still have some pull in this parish."

"Do you live here?" she asked, taking his warning to heart. "The name I had for this address is S. Sheridan."

"The house belonged to my wife," the sheriff explained. "Never had the title changed when we got married. Never needed to worry about that. But then, that's not why you're here, is it?"

Alice swallowed back the dread that had

drained all the air from her lungs. She'd come this far. Now she needed to find out the whole story. And from the look on Old Man Guidry's face, she didn't think she was going to like it.

Jonah looked over the stack of permits and contracts one more time, thinking he really needed to bring down someone from the home office to be his assistant. Especially now that things were going strong and this looked like a reality, not just a plan. Everything was right on schedule with the park and the model home. All the bids from local contractors were in, and he was just about set to start building the entire complex. Both the local government and the parish government had approved the development tracts, so he'd be able to get the entire infrastructure in place, hopefully by the first of next year. And he had signed real estate contracts and title transfers for the bulk of the land he'd managed to buy. Meanwhile, he had his people back in Shreveport working on the rest. He couldn't believe this would soon be a real community.

He looked out the window of his room at the inn and realized it was late afternoon.

Why hadn't Alice called him? He had to wonder if she was avoiding him again since they'd kissed.

How was he supposed to stay focused on this project when Alice was so front-and-center in his every waking thought? Maybe he'd walk over to the magazine office and see what she was up to. She'd told him she wanted to talk to him one more time before she filed her article about what she'd been calling the "Sheridan project."

"What *am* I going to call this?" he wondered out loud. The official government permits and myriad other papers showed it as JS Development. Was that what he wanted to name it? No, it needed a better name than the one he'd been stuck with, and he didn't just want his initials on the project. It needed a name that would show exactly what kind of community he hoped to create.

Names were important, after all. He should know.

He thought back to the newspaper clipping Alice had given him. Getting up, he found the copy lying by the stack of papers on his makeshift desk in the corner of the cozy little room. Picking it up, he stared down at the blurry image, then walked over to the nightstand and looked at the framed eight-by-ten sketch of Rosette House.

"What kind of life did you have here?" He wished he could just ask Esther that question. Would he ever have a chance? He accepted his mother had apparently left this place long ago, but why did she leave? What had driven her away? Poverty, loneliness, shame because of her pregnancy? He had to know. Then maybe he could understand why she'd felt it necessary to leave him in an orphanage.

Once he got the model house up and going and hired an on-site real estate agent to help sell the rest of the complex, he intended to take some time to resume the never-ending search for his mother. Or at least to finally find out the truth about her. And he just might let Alice help him with that. She'd already given him a link between Esther and the sketch he'd had with him for all these years. A solid link. But was he ready to let her take over and dig up all the ugliness of the past? He'd have to think about that.

As he stood there, looking out the window that gave a perfect view of this sleepy bayou town, he decided what he'd name the new development.

Bryson Branch.

It was perfect.

And…he'd talk to Alice first, but he wanted to name the park Esther's Place. That seemed like the right thing to do. If the locals approved. What did he care about their approval? He owned that land now. He could name it whatever he wanted. Because it might be his only connection with the mother he'd never known.

He went back to his papers and files, determined to get his mind back on business for now. He really needed to find someone to help with the interior of the house. Someone with a sense of style in keeping with the Creole influence of Rosette House. And then he remembered something Jay had said about Lorene wanting to be an interior designer. Maybe she could help him decide which color palettes to use.

And he was pretty sure she could help without getting out of her spot on the couch.

Alice looked up to see Dotty standing at the door of the conference room. "So, this is where you've been hiding out all day."

Alice nodded, blinking back the fatigue tugging at her burning eyes. "Sorry. I… needed a quiet spot to go over my notes. I'm supposed to meet with Jonah tonight to finish up the article. I should have it on your desk tomorrow morning."

Dotty slung a hip up onto the table, then started swinging one leg, her bright, orange high-heeled ankle boots shining in the dreary light. "Girl, you gotta level with me. Something is wrong and I want to know what it is so I can help."

Alice lowered her head. "I think I've made a mess of things, Dot."

"As in?"

When she didn't respond right away, Dotty lifted Alice's chin with one elegant finger. "Talk to me."

Alice put down her pen. "It's not the story, so don't worry about that. The story is accurate and fair. I'm almost finished, I promise."

Dotty crossed her arms against her stomach. "I'm not worried. You always deliver. Even when I nag you."

Alice smiled at that. "I do, don't I? I always snoop and ask questions and get to the bottom of things so I have all the facts, and then I write from the heart."

"Yeah, that just about sums you up."

"Yep, that's me. So good at my job. So thorough."

Dotty let out a groan. "You're killing me here, suga'. Just tell me what's wrong."

Alice got up to pour her third cup of coffee from the urn sitting on a nearby credenza. She needed to talk to someone and she couldn't burden Lorene with this, not now when her sister was so worried about her baby. Dotty was always willing to listen and she never, ever repeated anything Alice told her in confidence. "I've been doing some research for Jonah on the side—nothing involving the article. It's more…personal."

Dotty glanced around, then got up to shut the door. "Go ahead, I'm listening."

Alice looked down at her black coffee. "Jonah never knew his mother. He was left in an orphanage—a children's home—when he was five, and then later when he was a teen, he lived in a foster home. One of the reasons he came here specifically to develop this land is because he traced his biological mother back to Bayou Rosette."

Dotty's dark eyebrows lifted. "Really, now?"

"Yes," Alice said. "But none of this is going in the article, understand. And it's not to leave this room."

"Got it." Dotty lifted a hand. "Tell me more."

"He's pretty sure his mother was Esther Mayeaux."

"Oh, boy. I've heard some things about the Mayeaux."

"Yeah, oh, boy. He didn't have much to go on. His father wasn't listed on the birth certificate. But when he was left at the orphanage, he had a little suitcase with a few things in it. One of those things was a pen and ink sketch of Rosette House. Apparently, he's carried that sketch everywhere with him, so when he saw the reprint of my piece in the New Orleans paper a few months ago...well, he got this idea to come here and find out the truth while he helped rebuild the community."

Dotty shot off the desk. "Get outta here."

"I know," Alice replied. "I couldn't believe it, either. I haven't seen the sketch, but I did find an old newspaper clipping where Esther Mayeaux won an art contest in middle school. She won with that sketch, Dotty. The very same sketch Jonah has carried with him all of his life. It's his only link to his mother and when he saw the actual house in the newspaper article, he started out on this quest to find out the truth. So he came up with this idea for developing the land around the bayou and he invested heavily in making this new subdivision become a reality, all because he believes he has roots here."

"Roots stemming from the notorious Mayeaux clan," Dotty retorted. "How'd he take that, anyway?"

"He's okay with that, I think. In spite of all the legendary things he's read and heard about her older brothers, he couldn't find out much about Esther." She stopped, put a hand to her mouth. "But, of course, I couldn't leave things alone."

"So you did find something, right?" Dotty asked, her gaze holding Alice's. "Child, what on earth did you stumble across to have you in such a tizzy?"

Alice sank down on her seat, the sick feeling inside her stomach causing her insides to recoil and roil. "Things I wish I'd never heard," she said on a dry whisper. "Things I can never print."

Dotty touched her hand. "What kind of things?"

Alice looked up at her friend. "Dotty, you have to promise you won't mention this to anyone, okay?"

"Okay, but you're scaring me, honey. What is it?"

Alice took a deep breath. "Esther Mayeaux

allegedly had an affair with a married man. He was older and he lived up in Century, Louisiana."

Dotty nodded. "Okay. It happens." Then she let out a whistle. "Is this man Jonah's father?"

"I think so," Alice said, looking down at the table. "His name was Sonny Sheridan... and he was the stepson of Sheriff Samuel Guidry."

Dotty let go of Alice's hand. "Oh, no. Guidry had far-reaching power back in the day, from what I heard when I first came here."

"Oh no is right," Alice agreed. "That man was very powerful before he finally got voted out of office."

"Yep, sure was. So what's the official story?"

"I talked to the retired sheriff today," Alice admitted. "Off the record, as I promised him over and over, since he threatened me with all kinds of dire repercussions if I printed anything. It took some sweet-talking and convincing, but he told me his version of things—and threatened me within an inch of my life if I wrote about it. He's dying, so he only agreed to talk to me to finally ease his own conscience, I think. He said Sonny and Esther were having a fling but when Sonny tried to break it off, Esther accused Sonny of date-rape. She tried to go public and have him arrested, but that didn't work out."

"Oh, my." Dotty shook her head. "And let me guess why. No one believed her over the powerful sheriff and his stepson, so she never had her day in court?"

"It never got as far as anyone ever believing her, although this is the reason she left," Alice said. "Esther went to the locals for help, but instead of investigating, they immediately reported things to the sheriff in the next parish—knowing Sonny was his stepson. Esther was probably trying to keep it from her father and brothers, but the sheriff called her in and shut her up with threats before she could ever accuse Sonny publicly. According to the retired sheriff, he didn't believe her story, so he managed to hush her up and stop the rumors—probably through more threats and intimidation. He said her daddy and brothers came to him and Sonny intent on blackmail, but somehow he held them off—and kept this quiet for over thirty years, apparently. And he did it by buying out the Mayeaux. He gave them a large check and told them to leave this area, but he never did anything with the land. Later, he sold their land and made a tidy profit on it, from the way he talked. So this is why no one's heard anything or seen them all this time. He paid them off and told them to get out of Louisiana."

"So Jonah's mother was pregnant when she left?"

"That's about the gist of it. But Sonny Sheridan is dead. He was killed in a motorcycle accident years ago," Alice replied. "Sheriff Guidry didn't mention a baby, so I didn't dare tell him that Esther had a son. But at least now I know how Jonah got the Sheridan name. His mother gave that as his official name when she dumped him at the orphanage. Even though his father wasn't named on the birth certificate, she gave him the name Jonah Sheridan."

"Why did she leave him there at the orphanage?" Dotty asked, her brow furrowed.

Alice shook her head. "That's the one question I can't seem to find an answer for, and I couldn't ask the sheriff to clarify things since he's clueless, or so he seemed. But I intend to find out. I'm going to find Esther Mayeaux and get to the bottom of this. I have to, for Jonah's sake. And somehow, I have to tell him what I've found."

Dotty rubbed a hand across her face. "That might not be such a good idea, suga'."

"What do you mean? He has to know the truth."

"Are you sure?" Dotty asked, her dark eyes penetrating Alice's numb shock.

"I'd want to know," Alice replied. "He needs to know so he can just…get on with things." She couldn't admit it to Dotty, but she was so afraid Jonah would bolt if all of this was accurate. And she didn't want him to go away.

Dotty shook her head. "Or maybe the best thing he can do is let this go, once and for all."

"I can't believe you're suggesting that. You're the one who taught me the truth has to be told."

Dotty leaned over the table, her eyes bright with regret. "Trust me, honey, some things are best left unsaid. Sometimes the truth is much worse on a person than not knowing."

"But—"

"Alice, baby, please listen to me. Why do you think I left New Orleans, anyway?"

"I have no idea," Alice said, wondering what other revelations she was about to discover.

"A man, honey. It's always about a man," Dotty said. "I fell fast and hard and I wound up in the same shape as Esther, poor and pregnant. Then later on, I got married and had a pretty good life until I decided to go messing in the past. I wanted things between my new husband and me to be on an even keel, so I was blunt and told him the whole truth—that I had a child and gave that child up for adoption."

Seeing Alice's gasp of shock, she shook her head. "Yeah, he was shocked to hear that, too. I expected him to accept things, though, and help me find my child. But he turned cold and angry. A few weeks later, I found out I was pregnant again and I was so happy, thinking our baby would soften him. But it was too late. He dumped me before I could tell him about the baby, and I lost my baby—had a miscarriage after he left me high and dry, not only pregnant but holding the steep loan payment on our publishing company. And we were *married* and happy, except for the part about him not liking my past. I thought I could fix the past. But my man didn't want any part of that. And so, he left me."

She rubbed her hands together as if she were freezing cold. "I can't tell you how many times I wished I'd never gotten pregnant, wished I'd never told him about the baby I gave up. If I'd just left things alone, I might not have had the miscarriage."

She leaned back on the table, staring off into space. "I hate myself for what I did. And I can't forgive him. He didn't even care enough to see how I was doing. After he divorced me, I had nothing, nothing at all. So I had to come here and start over from scratch." She shrugged as if she'd just told Alice she had a headache. "So I'm telling you from experience, Jonah might be better off not knowing the truth. It's just too painful sometimes. And no amount of prayer or hoping can change the ugliness of the past. I don't believe God can ever make me feel better about myself."

Alice had to catch her breath. "Dotty, I had no idea. I'm so sorry."

Dotty held up a hand. "I never talk about it and I don't want it mentioned again. It's over and I learned a hard lesson. I just wish I'd had the gumption to fight for my babies. Both my babies."

Alice sat still, shocked at Dotty's story. Shocked but filled with a strong understanding of why Dotty hid behind that wall of toughness. She wanted to reach out to Dotty and tell her that prayer would help her. And that God could heal her. Instead, she just stared up at her friend, wondering if maybe Dotty was right. *Would* Jonah be better off knowing the truth? Or would the ugliness of it just make things all that much harder for him? Especially if she had to be the one to tell him?

How could she show him that God had brought him here for a reason? Maybe that reason was so he could let go of the past, rather than try to find it.

"What should I do, Dotty?"

"Leave it alone," her friend said. "If Jonah wants to know the rest of the story, let him find it out on his own. That's the best advice I can give you."

Then Dotty turned and walked out the door.

Chapter Thirteen

"Alice, come and see!"

At the sound of her sister's excited voice echoing through the house, Alice dropped her purse and hurried through the door. "Where are you?"

"In the den," Lorene called. "In my usual spot."

Alice rounded the kitchen counter, relieved to see Lorene's smiling face peeking over the couch.

"You scared me," she said. "Are you all right?"

"I'm great," Lorene replied as she sat up on her cushions. "Just resting until you got here."

Then Alice saw several wallpaper books and carpet and floor samples lying scattered here and there around Lorene. "Oh, my. Are you going to redo the whole house just out of boredom?"

"These aren't for our house," Lorene said on a giggle. "They're for Jonah's model house."

"What?" Alice sank down on the ottoman across from Lorene, her gaze scanning the pretty greens and pale yellows of the paint samples. "What are you doing with them?"

"He called me, asking for decorating advice," Lorene said, beaming with pride. "He told me he just needed me to look over these and put something together. No pressure and no getting up or straining myself."

Alice lifted one of the thick wallpaper sample books. "These things are heavy."

"I've been extra careful," Lorene replied. "I had Jay put them all right here within reach."

"Jay approved this?"

"He didn't seem so sure of the idea when he first came home and found Jonah and me poring over this stuff, but when he saw how excited I was...well, he caved. As long as I rest and as long as I don't walk across the bayou to supervise anything, both Jay and the doctor said it was okay."

"Good advice, since you can barely walk into the kitchen."

Lorene patted her stomach. "I love this baby and I'm gonna make sure he makes it into this world, you don't have to worry about that. But this…this is so much fun!" She held up a swatch of fabric. "It's something I've always wanted to do and now Jonah's letting me do it. And…he's paying me a reasonable salary. That will sure help with hospital bills and baby supplies."

Alice didn't know what to say. "That was awfully nice of him, to think of you. You're perfect for this."

"I think I am," Lorene said with a confident grin. "And I have no idea how he knew. Did you mention it to him—about me wanting to be an interior designer?"

"I don't think so," Alice said, getting up to pour a glass of water. "I did tell him about you never going to college—you know, the whole story."

"You mean the story where you think I sacrificed everything so you could get a college education?"

Alice looked over at her sister and saw the smile on Lorene's face. "Yes, that story."

"You know I don't care about all that," Lorene said. "I have everything I want right here. But you and Jay seem to want to make me out to be more of a martyr than I really am." She leaned forward, her smile as glowing as the late-afternoon sunlight streaming through the windows. "I didn't sacrifice anything, Alice. I chose something I loved—my husband and my home. You're the one who insisted on coming back here after college, when we both know you had big dreams of your own, so just get over that notion of me being the giving one, okay?"

"Okay, let's call it even. I came back because I wanted to. I'm happy here." Alice put her empty glass in the sink and came back into the den. "But you did give up a lot for me. I don't think Jay has to feel guilty, but I sure do."

"Which is why you might have mentioned this in passing to Jonah, right?"

"I didn't, I promise," Alice said. "I haven't talked to him much in the last couple of days."

"He told me you two are seeing each other later tonight."

"Yes, we're supposed to." She pushed at her hair. "I have to finish up the article."

Lorene's smile changed to a frown. "Are you all right?"

Alice couldn't put a damper on Lorene's

joy, so she nodded. Her sister didn't need to know the details of Jonah's parentage. "I'm okay. I just had a long day at work and I've got to burn the midnight oil to get this story in. Dotty's on the warpath."

"Isn't she always?" Lorene asked. "Come sit with me and let me show you all these pretty colors for the model house. That'll cheer you up."

"You're right. I think that will help. I can't wait to see the finished house."

Lorene pointed to a sample book. "Bring that one over here. I like the light greens for the kitchen and living room and maybe some earth tones for the den. It's a three-bedroom with two baths, but when Jonah showed me the plans, I couldn't help but notice the similarities."

Alice leaned forward to study the printout of the house plans lying on the table. "What similarities?"

Lorene looked surprised. "He said you'd seen this. Look at it. This house is like a miniature version of Rosette House."

Alice grabbed the floor plans. "What do you mean?"

Lorene bobbed her head. "It's more modern and not quite as square and wide and it does have certain 'green' stipulations, but this house has a lot of the same features as ours. I think that's kind of a sweet tribute, don't you?"

Alice stared down at the plans. "Yes, that is sweet. I glanced over the original plans but I didn't see the connection."

"This is a revised version," Lorene replied. "I'm telling you, you don't have to doubt Jonah's intentions. He's so thorough and so confident that he's doing the right thing, I have no worries that he's going to build the best community he possibly can. This means a lot to him."

Alice swallowed back the lump in her throat. "Yes, it does mean a lot to him. I know that now. I can see it clearly in this beautiful house."

"And I get to decorate it," Lorene said. "Well, at least from a distance. But he did tell me that after the baby comes and if I'm up to it, I can work for him part-time, here from home. He wants me to oversee the interiors of all the houses. I still can't believe he's trusting me to do this."

Alice certainly could believe it. Jonah was way more trusting with people than she'd ever been, even though he had a way of holding himself back from getting involved. And that was probably why he built houses. He could provide people with beautiful homes and live vicariously through them, without putting his own heart out there on the line.

Now he'd offered her sister the dream she'd always held in her heart. How could Alice not fall for a man who was that considerate and kind?

"I'm happy for you," she told Lorene. "Just don't overdo things, okay?"

"I won't, I promise," Lorene said. "All I have to do is pick out the colors and coordinate everything. I can do that sitting still right here. This will keep me busy for the next few weeks. And by the time I have the baby and I'm back on my feet, the little one and I can walk over and see what's going on. Won't that be great?"

"It's wonderful," Alice said, her joy for her sister overriding her concern for Jonah. "I'll go get dinner started. I thought I'd make us a salad and grill some chicken. And we have those fresh squash Paulette brought by. I can sauté them with some sweet onions. I think I can cook all that without burning the house down."

"Sounds great," Lorene said, her attention on the samples lying around her. "Thanks, honey."

Alice went across into the big kitchen, glad

that Lorene had something to focus on until the baby came. She heard the back door open and smiled as Jay walked in. "She's having a blast," she said in a low voice.

"I know," Jay said, grinning. "She was so excited when I came in earlier and found Jonah here. I was worried, but I think she can handle this, don't you?"

"Of course she can," Alice replied. "I just can't figure how Jonah found out about her talents."

Jay scratched his head, then looked over at his wife. "I might have dropped a hint to him the other day."

Surprised, Alice stared over at her brother-in-law. "Did you, now? Jay Hobert, I never knew you could be that innovative. Good thinking."

"I just want my wife to have everything," he said, suddenly shy again. "I wasn't so sure it would happen this fast when I mentioned it to Jonah, but then today when I came in and saw her so happy, I knew she'd be perfect for the job. And we called the doctor for approval."

"So you pretended to protest just to throw her off the trail, huh?"

He looked sheepish. "Yeah, something like that. Don't tell now, okay?"

"I wouldn't dream of it. She's acting like a kid in a candy store."

"Yeah, it's good to see her smiling."

"You are a very wise man," Alice said, giving him a gentle tap on his arm.

"Hey, what are you two cooking up over there?" Lorene called out.

"Oh, nothing, sweetheart," Jay replied. "Just some squash."

Alice laughed as she shooed him out of the kitchen. "Go in there and help her get all that stuff organized. And make sure she doesn't get too overworked."

"I won't let that happen," Jay said. "I just want to enjoy that pretty smile on her face."

Alice watched as Jay hugged her sister close, her own heart leaping at the pure love they shared for each other. Lorene was glowing in spite of having to stay inside and off her feet. And Jay's eyes shined with a deep, abiding love. Why couldn't everyone have that kind of love?

As she cut up vegetables and made tea, Alice had to wonder if she'd ever experience the joy of marriage and children. She thought of Jonah and what she needed to tell him and her heart shattered in grief.

The picture she saw of her sister and Jay

was a brilliant contrast to the picture she had in her mind of Jonah's mother and all that she'd possibly suffered.

How did you tell the man you were falling in love with that his father could turn out to be a monster?

Jonah turned off the engine of his car and got out. He walked toward the back door, then stopped to look through the big, wide windows of Rosette House, his heart filling with a kind of odd warmth. Jay and Lorene were sitting close together and laughing. The glow from a nearby lamp shone down on them like a halo, giving them a golden-washed aura. Lorene, reclining on two white ruffled pillows, pointed to the fabric samples on her lap, while Jay nodded and grinned.

It was good to know he'd been a part of making Lorene smile, of giving her a sense of purpose while she waited these last few weeks for her baby to be born.

Jonah watched the happy couple for a minute, then looked over toward the other side of the big room, past the wide granite counter, where through another window he could see Alice busy in the kitchen. She threw some sliced squash into a big pan, then stirred things around, her eyes downcast, her hair pulled back in that haphazard way with a bright orange clip. He watched as she glanced over at her sister and Jay, and he saw the tinge of remorse and regret in her eyes. He saw the bittersweet smile that just touched her lips.

Jonah stood there, his heart lifting up and out, as he wished a thousand times over he knew how to truly love someone. But he'd never been given the gift of unconditional love from family, so he wasn't sure what it really felt like to offer that same gift. Was this it? This pounding in his temple, this tightening in his chest? This overwhelming need to cherish and protect and fight for someone else? He'd loved Aunt Nancy because she was so easy to love. But something had always held him back from giving in to that need for a deep, abiding, forgiving love.

Until now.

He let out a caught breath and started for the door.

And just as he reached it, Alice looked up and out into the dusk, her gaze locking with his. Her smile was tempered with all the doubt and trepidation Jonah felt right now. And he had a feeling she was battling the same emotions he kept pushing away. But she dropped what she was doing and rushed toward the door. Then she held it open and said, "Come in."

Jonah walked toward her, knowing he was taking a path that he might never be able to turn away from again. And while he hoped he wouldn't regret it, he also prayed that this time he'd land in a place he never wanted to leave.

Chapter Fourteen

Two hours later, Jay and Lorene had gone to bed and Alice and Jonah were finishing up the dishes.

"You didn't have to help," Alice said, glad that he was going to stay awhile so they could go over the last-minute details of the article. She loved being with Jonah, but she was on edge about what she'd found out about his past. How could she tell him?

During the meal, she hid her worries with small talk about the house Lorene would help decorate. It had been easy to put aside the dark thoughts clouding her judgment and bask in the glow of Lorene's newfound excitement and Jonah's growing enthusiasm. But now that they were alone, she didn't know how to tell him the truth. And she wasn't so sure what the truth was anymore. Or if telling him was the right thing to do.

"I don't mind helping," he said as he handed her the dish towel. "But…you don't seem so sure. I thought we had some things to discuss, unless you're too tired."

"No, I'm not tired." She shrugged. "Well, I mean, I am tired but I always get this way right before a deadline. Nothing new there."

"Are you worried about Lorene? I won't let her overdo things with being my consultant. And Jay will make sure of that, too. Just a couple of hours a day, and the doctor backed that up."

"No, I'm happy for Lorene. This is exactly what she needs to keep her distracted. And she won't put her baby in jeopardy. I'm okay with that."

His brow furrowed. "Are you worried about this article, then? I can handle any and all observations, you know. I'm tough."

"I believe you are," she replied, praying that was so. "But the article is fair and accurate—not too much to fret about there. It should bring you a lot of possible homeowners. Let's go up to my place and… we'll get this done, once and for all."

He followed her through the front door and up the wide outside staircase, then reached for her hand when they got to the upstairs porch. "It must be me, then. Are you tired of me already?"

She didn't know how to answer that. Normally, she would have blurted out the truth—no, she wasn't tired of him. But tonight, she was all twisted inside, in turmoil about what to tell him, how to tell him, about what she'd found out. "I said I'm tired, but that doesn't mean I'm tired of *you.* I think we're making progress, you and me."

Or at least, they had been until she'd managed to dig up too much of his past. *Give me courage, Lord,* she silently prayed. Jonah had asked her not to pry, but it was too late to go back now.

"I'll say we're making progress. We've definitely rounded a curve." He touched a finger to her loose curls. "Your hair is cute that way."

She drew back but smiled up at him. "Lorene calls this my after-work hairdo."

"Well, you do automatically reach for a clip the minute you get home."

She turned, one hand on the door to her apartment. "And how would you know that, Jonah Sheridan?"

He pointed out across the bayou. "Because I watch you sometimes, from over there."

Alice looked to where a single yellow security light glowed against a construction trailer. "You watch me? You spying on me, Jonah?"

"Not spying—the way *some* people do." He grinned at that. "I just like watching you and being around you. And when I hear that doodlebug coming up the lane, I can't help but glance up. I mean, the thing does clank and clunk its way around town."

"Okay, so my car is noisy. Which is why I parked so far away from Mr. Gauthier's cabin when I *was* spying on you. What other excuses do *you* have for spying on me?"

He leaned close, one hand going on the doorjamb. "I said, I like watching you. It's that simple. You make me smile."

Alice sank back against the screen door. "Can't say I've ever heard that one before. Most people run from me in terror."

"I almost did," he admitted, his hand slipping back to her hair. "But I'm glad I didn't."

Almost. There was that word again.

Alice knew he was going to kiss her and so she leaned toward him. She needed to know he felt the same as she did. Just for now, just for tonight.

He lowered his head, his lips touching cheek. "You smell like squash."

That made her laugh and, when she did, he grabbed her giggle inside a kiss that turned from playful to serious. "I like squash," he said as he lifted away.

"That's good. Now cut it out and come on inside so we can get this story put to bed. Because once I'm finished with this, we can get on with…being friends."

His eyes were a smoky gray. "Friends, Alice? Is that what you want from me?"

She wanted a lot, but right now she was afraid to voice those wants. "For now, that would be a good start, don't you think?"

"I can't complain. Considering you weren't so sure about me when we met."

"I've warmed up to the idea of having you around," she said as she pushed through the door and flipped on the lights.

"Good, because I just might stick around."

That caused her to do a spin. "Really? As in, visit for a while or actually move here?"

He looked down at all her notes and files then back up and into her eyes. "I'm thinking about moving here and staying here for a long time."

Alice tried to hide the little jolts of excitement coursing through her pulse. "I guess we do kind of grow on people—the charming small-town life and all that."

"It's not just the small-town life, Alice. I want the life itself. I want *a* life. I've never had that."

Her heart melted at that admission. "But you've accomplished a lot. You managed to go to college, start your own company. You're a self-made man. You should be proud."

He shrugged. "Maybe, but I've been going through the motions, trying to run from my past at times, and at other times trying to find my past. It's like I've been caught in this vicious cycle, spinning but never actually getting anywhere." He looked over at her, his eyes going soft. "And then I came here—with a purpose and that underlying hope of finally getting the answers I needed. And in the process, I've turned back to my faith, Alice. I've turned a corner and I think it's all right here. All the answers I've been searching for so long, all the questions I had about trusting in God—it's all right here. I'm thinking now it's not so much about my past, but more about my future. With you."

Alice had to look away. His words echoed the very prayer she'd sent up to God so many times since she'd grown closer to Jonah. How could she tell him the truth now? How could she shatter that delicate thread of hope she saw in his eyes? She was falling for him and she'd like nothing better than to keep him here, but...if she told him the truth he'd leave. She knew he'd leave because she was beginning to know *him* and how he'd react.

She knew why he always stood just outside the door before entering each time he came to Rosette House. He'd had that image of a home in his mind since an early age. But in his mind, just as in the picture he'd carried with him, he was always standing outside of the perimeter, just outside of the kind of life he'd always needed. And now, she had invited him in. And by doing so, she'd somehow found the courage to heal her own broken heart and learn to hope again. Her hope was in Jonah now. And in her own growing faith and Jonah's calming presence.

But if he found out the ugliness of what might have happened with his parents, he'd leave Bayou Rosette and never come back. That elusive picture he'd carried in his mind and in his heart would be tainted with tragedy and sadness. And he'd always blame her for forcing him to see the truth.

An hour later, Jonah finished reading the pages in front of him, then looked up to find Alice pacing in the cozy sitting room of her apartment.

"What do you think?" she asked as he let out a long breath.

"I think you're a very good journalist," he responded, meaning it. "You were thorough, accurate with the research about building green and you somehow managed to explain all my hopes and dreams for this development without making me sound like a greedy land developer. And you left my personal life out of it, thank goodness."

She whirled at that. "Well, your personal life wasn't the focus of this article. This story is business, pure and simple, and it's about something that will be good for this town. I can't see anyone thinking any differently, regardless of what I write."

He leaned back against his chair, his gaze on her. "But what about you, Alice? What do you think, now that it's all been laid out in front of you?"

She came over to the table then pressed her hands on the smooth wood. "I think this town is blessed to have you, that's what I think. A blessing in disguise, that's what you are. And I think your aunt Nancy was right. You're a gift. You have a gift—to create beautiful places, to build solid homes that good, solid people can afford to live in."

He shook his head. "While that's all fine and good, I need to know what you think… about me as a person."

"I just told you."

"You complimented me but you didn't tell me how you feel…about us. About me."

She pushed away from the table, a darkness filling her eyes. Maybe she didn't feel the same as he did. "Alice?"

"There's still so much…between us," she said, her voice low, her head down. "But… we're getting there. We've got time."

"I know what you said earlier—we're making progress. But *progress* is something a developer would say. I want something more personal, something more intimate to describe what's happening between us."

When she didn't answer, he got up to

pull her around. "Unless you're having second thoughts. Have I been reading things wrong here?"

"No, you're not reading anything wrong. But I have concerns. A lot of concerns."

He stood back, disappointed but trying to understand. "You're still afraid of being hurt again?"

She lifted her head. "Yes, but…I'm also afraid you'll get hurt."

That comment perplexed him. "Are you planning on hurting me?"

"Not if I can help it."

"Then tell me what's bothering you."

Her smile was almost apologetic. "You still have a lot of things to work through."

"You mean, regarding my mother?"

"Yes. I know you don't want me to interfere—"

"It's not about that," he said, understanding dawning. "I don't mind that you helped me make a connection with her. It's just that I think this is something I have to finish, one way or another, on my own. I have to do it—it's my problem to solve."

"And what if you don't like what you find?"

"I'll just have to deal with that when the time comes," he said, wondering why she was so centered on this now. Was she grasping at things to keep them apart?

Hoping to reassure her, he pulled her close. "Just let me worry about all of that, okay? Right now, I want to enjoy being here with you. We've pushed through some major hurdles, Alice. When we met out there on the bayou, we both had a lot of baggage. You wanted to punish me for what Ned Jackson did to you, and I tried to place you as a roadblock to accomplishing what I'd set out to do here. But I'm not like Ned and I think you can see that now. And…you weren't out to do me in or cause me to get run out of town on a rail. You were just protecting the place and the people you love."

He lifted his hands, then let them drop by his side. "And look at us now. The things we thought were holding us back are gone, all cleared up. Look how far we've come in the past few weeks. Not only am I going to build this new community, but you seem to be behind me all the way." Then he tugged her back into his arms. "And…I've found a link to my mother, a link that will guide me through getting these homes built. I'll have her image front and center every time I break ground on a new foundation. No matter what

I find out from here on out, I'll always have that image, thanks to you." He gave her a peck on the cheek. "Don't you think that's pretty cool?"

She bobbed her head. "I think it's wonderful. Almost too wonderful. I'm—"

"You're waiting for the other shoe to drop, for something bad to happen? Well, stop waiting." He kissed her again. "Nothing is going to happen, because now there is nothing standing between us. All those obstacles weren't the real issue, Alice. The real deal is how we feel about each other. It's down to you and me now. Just you and me."

Her eyes grew misty as she gazed up at him. And her next words floored him. "Well, maybe that's the part that scares me the most."

She couldn't sleep. The gold-etched porcelain clock on her nightstand told Alice it was close to three in the morning. She had always cherished the hazy memories of her mother and father, but now she could almost hear her mother's voice, soft and whispery against her ear as she tucked Alice back into bed after a nightmare. "It's always still and scary this time of night, but there's nothing to fear. Christ is watching over you, always."

Alice didn't know why a single tear moved down her cheek. She thought of her parents every day, but this particular memory seemed so real, so close. And she prayed that Christ was watching over her, but more so, she asked the Lord to watch over Jonah and help him. "He's going to need You," she whispered. "And I'm going to need You…after I tell him."

Jonah thought they'd gotten through the worst. He believed they now had a chance to be together, to have a future. And she wanted to believe that, too.

But how could she? She'd wanted to tell him about his father, about the allegations his mother had tried to bring up, but she'd watched his handsome face, had seen the soft smile there, the light of hope and joy in his eyes. And she just couldn't bring herself to shatter all that hope and joy. Not yet.

"You blew it," she said to herself. "You panicked and you chickened out."

Now, somehow, she was going to have to tell Jonah what she'd done. Somehow, she wanted to make him see that they could get past this one last obstacle. If everything Sheriff Guidry had told her was true, then Jonah could find his mother and get to the truth at last.

If only he'd stay around long enough to do that, after Alice explained her findings to him.

But would he? That was the question keeping her from finding any rest tonight. And even her mother's hushed assurances moving through her memories couldn't help. So she lay there in the darkness, in the stillness, and she listened to the silence, a great loneliness weighing on her soul. And she prayed that God was listening, too.

Chapter Fifteen

"Let's go on a date."

Alice held her cell phone to her ear, Jonah's soft words radiating through her fatigue. "A date?" She leaned back in her office chair. "Hmm. We've never actually been on one of those, have we?"

He laughed. "No, and from what I've heard, that's how most couples get to know each other. I was thinking a nice picnic out on the bayou."

"A picnic? I haven't been on a real picnic since—" She stopped, swallowing back all the bitterness and regret in her soul. "Since before my parents died."

"Oh, if it's a bad idea—"

"No, no. I think it's a great idea." She turned to find Dotty's radar gaze centering on her. "What time?"

"Can you get off a bit early, say around five?"

"I can probably do that. Where?"

"I'll meet you at the park across from your house."

"Oh, you mean the park that you're building?"

"That's the one. I might call it Esther's Place."

Alice let that soak in, her stomach clutching at all she knew about Esther. "I like that," she said, her tone whisper soft.

"Okay. When you get there, I'll tell you the name for the subdivision, too."

"I'll be there. Do I need to bring anything?"

"No. Paulette and I have planned everything. Just bring your pretty self."

"Okay. See you then."

Alice hung up then stared at Dotty. "What?"

"You haven't told him yet, have you?"

Alice shook her head. "I can't seem to find the right time."

"You've had all weekend."

"I avoided him all weekend," she admitted. "I told him I was tired from getting this issue of the magazine to bed. And that I wanted to stick close to Lorene, since Jay needed to get some things finished in the fields before winter sets in."

"Both good excuses, but you could have met with him, all the same."

Alice got up, lifting her hands in the air. "Okay, so I'm a coward. I don't want to be the one to cause him any more pain, Dotty. You said I shouldn't tell him anyway, remember?"

Dotty slanted her head, her gold hoop earrings sparkling against her ears. "I understand that, suga', and yes, I tried to talk you out of it, but you've always been so brutally blunt. This isn't like you. You owe it to that man to level with him."

"Well, you've sure changed your tune."

"I know," Dotty replied. "But...I told *my* husband about giving up my baby. You'd be telling Jonah something he's been trying to figure out all his life. I think there's a difference. And since you found out the story, you need to be the one to tell him."

"You're right, I do. But I also owe him a little time to just enjoy what he's accomplished. He needs this time. And even though he's already told me he wants to keep looking for his mother—and the truth—he also said he needs to finish his work here first. He can't do both at once, Dotty. Because he knows he'll need all his energy and time to pursue this. And…I think deep down inside he wants to be able to walk away, if it comes to that. He can't leave until he finishes what he started here."

"Which is the development? Or finding his past? Or maybe being with you?"

"All of the above. But as for the development and his past—he has to finish one before he can focus on the other. As for him and me—if I tell him this now, I don't know what will happen with us. I'm afraid he'll resent me so much there won't be any more us."

"You're in a real pickle, sweetheart."

"Tell me something I don't know. I worried about this all weekend. And I even tried to track down his mother—I looked on genealogy sites and searched old newspapers at the library on Saturday. And I plan to look up death records. She might not even be alive anymore, for all we know."

"But the man told you to cease and desist on the search."

"He did. But…I'm a lot like Jonah. I have to finish what I started. I opened this can of worms and now I have to find the truth, so I can be prepared when I finally tell him."

"Are you thinking of sitting on this for… months, years, maybe? 'Cause it might take that long for him to finish building that subdivision."

"I know," Alice said, getting up to pace the floor. "And I haven't decided. I don't know what to do. And you know that isn't usually a problem for me."

Dotty chewed her lip. "No, you've always been decisive and quick-thinking, but I reckon this is different. This is personal."

Alice slapped a hand on the desk. "Yes, too personal. He asked me to back off and he thinks I have. Now I know this awful thing and it's killing me. I wish I'd listened to Jonah."

"Well, Thanksgiving is next week. Is he going back to Shreveport for the holidays?"

"I don't think so," Alice said, back to pacing again. "He doesn't have any family there. He's got coworkers and friends, but I think Jonah's a loner by nature. He might just stay here and work."

"What if you told him then?"

"You mean, ruin a nice holiday by spilling the beans about his parentage? Yeah, that'll go over great."

Dotty blocked her. "Stand still and listen, will you?"

Alice nodded, then let out a breath. "Okay, I'm listening."

"I'm thinking the holidays will provide a lull in the work out there on the bayou. He'll probably let people at least have time with their families for Thanksgiving. Why not use that time to talk to him, be honest with him and get it all out in the open?"

"And what if he bolts?"

"He might, but he has an obligation to the people counting on him. That could be the leverage he needs to work through this."

"Is that how you cope? By working all the time?" Alice asked, wondering how Dotty found her strength.

Dotty gave her a hard stare. "Pretty much. But then, I like to work. I'm not big on holidays."

Alice hated to hear that, but she could tell Dotty didn't want to talk about it. "Dotty, why don't you come to our house on Thanksgiving?"

Dotty lifted her dark brows. "Excuse me?"

"You know, the day where we eat too much turkey and dressing and then we top it off with pie and cake? I don't think you've ever been to our house for a meal. Why not now?"

"You're changing the subject, aren't you?"

"No, I'm trying to listen to your advice. You might be right. Just get it all over with and hope Jonah can see past his hurt enough to forgive me."

"And why would *me* being at your house for Thanksgiving help with this in any way?"

"I need you there," Alice said, hoping to convince her stubborn friend that she shouldn't be alone on the holiday.

Dotty actually blinked.

"What's wrong?"

"I...I just never heard anybody say that—to me—I mean."

Alice stared at her boss. "Dotty, we all need someone. I need you. You're my rock."

"Stop it," Dotty replied, wiping at her eyes. "I don't cry. You know I don't cry."

"Well, maybe you should try it sometimes. It helps." Alice reached for her. "And so does hugging a good friend."

Dotty hesitated a minute, then grabbed her and patted her on the back. "Okay, you got me. I'll come to dinner. Just for you. But don't make me cry again, you hear? And don't expect a lot of hugging, either."

"I hear," Alice said. "And I'll do my best to tell Jonah the truth, somehow." Then she stood back. "But today, I intend to put this out of my mind for a couple of hours and go on a real date with a real man. A picnic, of all things. He's a tad romantic, don't you think?"

Dotty was back to being tough and stubborn, even though she was still sniffing. "I'm thinking a lot of things but…you go on and have fun. I guess you two deserve a reprieve from all the drama, at least for a little while."

Alice hoped her friend was right. And she refused to let the dark clouds from Jonah's past ruin this beautiful fall afternoon. She'd do a bit more searching and digging, then she'd tell him everything next week.

And she'd see if he truly could deal with all of it—no, make that if they *both* could deal with all of it.

He had everything ready.

Jonah surveyed the plaid picnic blanket, then checked the basket Paulette had helped him pack. He'd tried to think of some of the foods Alice had always ordered at the Bayou Inn—grilled chicken, salad, fruit and chocolate bread pudding. The woman loved her chocolate bread pudding.

Paulette had tossed in some freshly baked bread and a jug of her famous mint tea, too. And she'd provided nice plates, utensils and two pretty goblets. Paulette was a romantic.

"Just feed her and smile at her," she'd advised Jonah. "Most women just want to feel special. Make her feel special, Jonah. And if you hurt her, I'll break your legs."

Yeah, Paulette sure was a romantic.

He didn't want to hurt Alice. He wanted to talk to her, to laugh with her, to find out what her favorite color was, to ask her which season she loved the best, to see what she thought about Lorene's choices for the model house. He had so many questions.

Being around Alice had softened his burning need to find his mother. He still wanted to do that, but now he knew he could take his time and do it right. He'd keep digging in his spare time, but a lot of that time might be occupied by a cute, curly-haired blonde, if he had his way.

He heard her car rumbling up the winding lane to her house, then watched as she got out and looked across the water. She waved, her hair lifting in the wind. "Hey, you."

"Hey, yourself," he called, liking the way

she tossed her tote bag on a chair on the porch, then started prancing toward him.

He watched her cross the old bridge, watched as her long denim skirt floated around her cowboy boots. She had on a lightweight mint-green jacket and a crisp white blouse. Alice knew how to throw clothes together.

She knew how to make things happen. She knew how to make his heart zoom and his head spin. He was in trouble, but he liked it.

She came across the bridge and he stood up to meet her. "You made it."

"I did." She looked down at the blanket and the basket. "What's all this?"

"As promised, this is our very own picnic. With all your favorites from the Bayou Inn."

She glanced over the plates and goblets and then peeked into the basket. "Is that chocolate bread pudding?"

"Freshly made this morning."

"God bless Paulette," Alice said. Then she turned to him. "And God bless you. I needed this today."

Jonah wasn't used to that kind of salutation. "I need some blessing, I reckon," he said as he invited her to sit down. "And I think…I've found it here."

She took the goblet full of tea he poured,

then lowered her head. "You don't like talking about God, do you?"

He stared over at her for a minute before answering. "I've never felt that close to Him. I know He's out there, but sometimes it seems He's just too far out of reach."

He saw the shadow of fear in her eyes. "Hey," he said, reaching for her hand. "I believe. I do. I just don't put forth much effort on my own behalf."

"Because you don't think you matter to Him?"

Jonah filled her plate and handed it to her. "Maybe not. I didn't matter to my parents."

She lowered her head again, her gaze downcast. "Lorene's faith is so centered and so strong. I envy her that. I'm like you, I guess. I believe but I don't make a big deal out of it. I don't put Him front and center the way my sister does. But lately, I can see that I need to do that very thing."

He chuckled. "We're a pair—out here on a romantic picnic and talking about religion."

"It's an important part of my life," she said. "Even if I'm not as devout as Lorene, I sure need Christ in my life. And I need Him now more than ever."

Jonah saw the trace of regret in her glance.

"Because of me? Does it bother you that my faith isn't so strong?"

Her smile was tinged with confusion. "Well, yes, of course, but I think you're working on that. You've been in church a couple of times in the last few weeks. It's a start."

"But...is that a deal breaker, between us?"

"No, it's not. I can't sit in judgment of you, Jonah. I'm just worried about...a lot of things."

He sank down beside her. "Hey, this was supposed to be a nice picnic, not a worry session."

"You're right. And this food is so good. Thank you."

She looked around. "I like what you've done with the place. When I was little, I used to come over here and pretend I was a princess searching for hidden treasure."

"You probably didn't find any. Maybe a few baby gators and snakes?"

She laughed at that. "Oh, I ran into a few critters. But this land was always just sitting here like a giant maze, begging me to explore. Whenever I was feeling lost or confused, I'd hurry across that old bridge and come over here and climb that big oak tree. I felt so small and hidden up there in those old branches. It was right here that I'd try to figure out my life."

"And did you?"

She shook her head. "No, not really. I'm still going through that maze. And meeting you has only confused me even more."

"Want to go sit in the tree?"

Her laughter made him feel so good. "No, I think I'm too big for that now. But being here with you is nice. Different, but nice. Thanks again for thinking of this. Oh, and tell me what you decided to name the subdivision."

"Bryson Branch," he said, waiting for her reaction.

Her smile was soft and slow. He'd expected that. But the tears that misted her eyes surprised him.

"Is that okay?"

"It's…so thoughtful," she said. "Lorene will like that."

"But do you like that name?"

She nodded, blinked away the moisture of her unshed tears. "I do. I like it a lot."

"Good." He turned to reach behind the big basket. "I forgot. I brought something to show you."

He watched as Alice dropped her plate and took the framed picture of Rosette House. "Is this—?"

"The one my mother sketched. Yes, it is. I wanted you to see it."

She stared down at the perfect rendition of her home, his fingers touching the frame. "Jonah, it's so pretty. She must have been very talented. She captured the house perfectly."

"Yes, she did. And thanks to that picture, I'm here now and I've seen the house myself. But I've also seen what my mother saw each and every day. I've seen a home, Alice. A real home."

She looked up at him, her eyes still misty, her expression shuttered. "Jonah, I—"

"No, don't say anything. Don't." He tugged her close. "Just know that I'm grateful to you and your family for letting me into your lives. I'm so grateful."

He kissed her then and heard the sound of her sigh. It seemed full of hope and resolve. She shifted to get closer, her food forgotten. Jonah lifted his head to stare over at her. "Are you cold?"

She lifted her chin. "A little. Not too much." Then she whispered, "Will you come for Thanksgiving dinner?"

Jonah's heart pounded with a burst of something he'd tried so long to hold back. It felt like a great wave of water washing over him, this feeling of being so full he couldn't contain himself. He'd never felt this before, this burning warmth that covered him with hope and security and need. Maybe because, just like his long-lost mother, he had never before been invited in, truly invited in by someone he cared about. "I'd love to come to Thanksgiving dinner."

"I'm cooking," she said on a giggle. "Just wanted to warn you."

"I don't think I've ever had your cooking, except for those amazing squash."

"Neither have I. Well, okay, yes, except for the few meals I've managed to cook for Lorene and Jay lately."

He kissed her again, just because her admission made him fall completely in love with her. And the dam on his emotions burst forth with that realization, allowing his heart to open at last to the hope he'd long held at bay.

"I can't wait," he said as he hugged her close and rocked her. They sat still and quiet then, watching the sun set with a bright, golden fire behind the old live oak.

Finally, Alice leaned forward. "Hey, how about some of that chocolate bread pudding?"

"Good idea." He reached for the pan—still

warm underneath the foil Paulette had wrapped it in.

Then Jonah heard a vehicle rumbling up the driveway across the bayou. Alice sat up, looking toward the house.

"I wonder who that is," he said.

"I don't know, maybe somebody bringing Lorene more food. The church ladies love to make casseroles."

They watched as an old man got out of a truck, the effort of climbing down out of the driver's seat making him slow and unsteady.

Alice let out a gasp then went pale.

"What's wrong?" Jonah asked. "Do you know him?"

At first, she didn't say anything, then she abruptly pulled away and got up to stare down at him, an apologetic look on her face. "I'm sorry, Jonah. So sorry. But I have to go."

Chapter Sixteen

Alice ran across the bridge, her pulse hitting against her temple each time her boots hit the splintered wood. What was Sheriff Guidry doing here?

She reached him before he could knock on the door. "Mr. Guidry?"

He pivoted, unsteady on his feet. "There you are. That woman in town told me I'd find you out here."

"What's the matter?" Alice asked, aware that Jonah was slowly making his way across the bridge.

Mr. Guidry's gaze held hers. He cleared his throat, held up a hand. "I need to know. I just need to know."

"Know what, sir?" Alice asked, praying

Jonah would stay away until she could figure out what the man wanted.

"My land—the land I bought from the Mayeaux—I told you I sold it to someone else."

"Yes, sir." Her mind started whirling. "But that was a while back, right?"

"Not that far back. A few months ago. I sold it to a corporation from up in Shreveport. A development company."

Alice thought she might be sick. Her stomach lurched as her world tilted. Why hadn't she seen this before? "You did? You never mentioned that."

"I didn't think I needed to. I didn't want to talk to you in the first place."

"This corporation—what's the name?"

"JS Building and Development," he said.

Alice swallowed, grabbed the porch-post. Mr. Guidry had sold the land he'd coerced from the Mayeaux family to his own step-grandson. She'd never even connected on that fact.

She looked up at him and then looked around at Jonah where he stood, waiting. "Why are you here?" she asked Mr. Guidry again.

"When you came to talk to me, I got curious about things. I wondered why you needed to know all of this now and I was worried that you'd print something, regardless of the facts. I called my lawyer and asked him to find out what was going on over here. And that's when he gave me a name…a name connected to JS Development. Jonah Sheridan. He told me there was a whole new community going up right across the bayou." He raised his voice with each word. "And I'm here now, young lady, to find out what kind of game you're playing with me. Did you know a Sheridan had bought that land from me the day you came and talked to me? You'd better tell me the truth right now. Did you know Jonah Sheridan bought that land?"

Alice looked from Mr. Guidry to Jonah, struggling to find air. "I—"

"Yes, she knew," Jonah said as he walked closer. "Who are you and what's going on here, anyway?"

Alice saw the awareness flare through Mr. Guidry's tired old eyes. He looked at Jonah, then stepped back, a hand going up. "You look like him," he said, his voice weak. "Just like him."

"Like who?" Jonah asked, his gaze moving between Alice and the old man.

Mr. Guidry turned to Alice. "Who is this man?"

"I'm Jonah Sheridan," Jonah said, stepping forward, his hand out, his expression wary. "Do I remind you of someone else, sir?"

"You sure do," Mr. Guidry said. "And I think I know why." He glared at Alice. "Is this why you came to see me?"

Alice couldn't speak, so she just nodded. "I'm not sure, but—"

"What are you talking about?" Jonah asked. He looked at Alice, lifting his eyebrows. "Talk to me."

Before Alice could speak, Mr. Guidry stepped forward. "You look like your father—Steven. Steven—we called him Sonny—Sheridan." Then he pointed toward Alice. "Didn't she tell you? He was my stepson. He loved Esther even though he was married. And he never knew anything about you. No one ever told us there was a baby involved."

Jonah heaved a breath, his gaze slamming into Alice's. "What does he mean? Alice, what's going on here?"

From inside the house, Lorene called out, "Alice, is everything okay out there?"

"We're fine," Alice said. "I'll be inside in a minute."

She looked at Jonah, her heart burning

with dread. "I did some more research on your parents, Jonah. And I found a Sheridan over in the next parish—in a town called Century. But when I got to the address, I—"

"She found me," Samuel Guidry said. "She found me and asked me all these questions—said she worked for a magazine here and she was just getting some background information. I thought she was trying to dig up lies to try and get something started up again, so I told her to leave us alone." He glared at Jonah. "Your daddy was hard to live with. He always resented me being the sheriff—wasn't happy when his mama and me got married. So he did everything in his power to get on my bad side. But I never had any children of my own, so I tried to do right by him."

Jonah barely moved, his resolved gaze on Alice. He looked calm but she could see the slight shaking of his whole body. "Go on."

Samuel leaned against a chair, then sank down. "But he truly loved your mother. He came to me, asking for help after…after she accused him. He was married, you see. Married to a good woman. He was trying to do better, but he loved your mama. It ain't true, what she claimed, even though she tried to convince me it was. It ain't true."

"And what did she claim?" Jonah asked, his tone measured and low, his gaze dark with dread. "Alice, what did my mother claim?"

Alice flinched at his words. "Jonah, I wanted to tell you. I was going to—"

"Tell me *now,*" he said, his voice rising. "Just tell me the truth. I deserve the truth—from both of you."

Alice looked at Samuel, then lifted her head. "Your mother claimed Steven Sheridan raped her, Jonah. And instead of helping her, Sheriff Guidry covered it up by buying out the Mayeaux so they'd leave Louisiana."

"It wasn't no cover-up!" Samuel Guidry shouted. "The accusations weren't true, that's all. She knew she was messing with a married man and when he wouldn't leave his wife to marry her, she turned ugly on him. I had to protect my wife and her son. I had to. I did the only thing I could. I sent 'em packing. And it all settled down. But now, all these years later, this girl here comes to my door and stirs it back up again." He hacked a cough. "I guess it's for the best. I could have died never knowing about you, but at least now I do. That's something good out of all of this." Then he pointed a finger at Alice. "But if you print a word of this, I'll make you regret it."

Jonah stood a few feet from the porch, shock and horror coloring his face. "And now I know the truth," he said, giving Alice a sharp-edged look. "Well, not the whole truth. I still don't know where my mother is. Or the man who hurt her. Where is my father?"

Mr. Guidry grunted. "Your daddy's dead, son. He died in a motorcycle accident about ten years ago. And I don't know about your mama. Don't know a thing about her."

Jonah lowered his head. "And you obviously don't care, do you?"

Samuel Guidry cleared his throat and looked up, his hands shaking. "I might have cared if I'd known. I might have made Steven own up to his responsibilities. But it's too late for that."

Jonah nodded his head, his jaw muscles tightening. "Yes, it's too late. Too late for both of us. The only justice here is that I now have my mother's land back. I have it and… I'm going to build something better over there, you hear me?" He pointed to the park. "It'll be better over there."

Alice went to him then. "Jonah, listen to me. I can help you—"

"Oh, you've helped me all right," he said, turning on her, his eyes flaring with fury.

"You've done so much for me, Alice. You went right on searching even when I told you to stop. Thanks for the offer, but no thanks. I think I can handle things from here."

Alice didn't know what to do to ease his hurt. "Jonah, come inside and we'll talk about it. I can help you find your mother. I can."

He pushed her away. "I have to get out of here. I have to think, to figure this out. I can't be here right now. I can't."

Mr. Guidry tried to stand. "What about me, son? Don't you want to talk to me?"

Jonah's hand sliced through the air. "I have nothing to say to you, old man. You could have helped her, but you refused to do that. You were a sheriff and you didn't even allow her to speak out. You didn't even try to find out the whole truth. Why on earth would I want to talk to you?"

He stalked off toward the bridge. Alice looked at Mr. Guidry. "I have to go and talk to him. Will you be all right?"

"I'm leaving," Mr. Guidry said, moving toward his truck. "I've had enough of this myself. I'm glad it's come to this. Glad he has his land back. At least I can die in peace now."

"Can you?" Alice asked, anger pouring through her. "You let his mother leave, not even considering that she might have been telling the truth. If I were you, I'd try to get that settled before you leave this earth."

With that, she stalked away toward the bridge, leaving the old man standing with one hand on his truck door.

She had to find Jonah right now and make him see that she was only trying to protect him. But even that excuse couldn't hide her shame or her regret. And she didn't think Jonah was going to believe it, either.

She'd made it to the foot of the bridge when she heard Jonah's truck roaring to life, followed by Lorene's scream. "Alice! Alice, help me. I think the baby's coming!"

Alice didn't hesitate. She started running toward the house, the sound of Jonah's pickup spewing dirt and rocks, its echo moving inside her fear for her sister.

"Is something wrong?" Mr. Guidry called from his truck.

"No, yes. I don't know," Alice called. "It's my sister. She's pregnant."

"I'll call nine-one-one," Samuel offered.

Alice nodded, then ran into the house to find Lorene.

* * *

Jonah slammed through the doors of the Bayou Inn, his only thought to get to his room and get packed. But Paulette stopped him on the stairs.

"Jonah, how'd the picnic go?"

"Not so good." He tried to push past her. "I have to go."

Paulette was petite but wide and she didn't seem in a hurry to get out of his way. "Did that man find Alice? I told him she was busy, but he insisted he needed to see her right away."

"Yeah, he found her."

"And?"

Jonah wasn't in the mood to talk about it. "I have to take care of something," he said. "Excuse me."

She let him pass, but he felt her hard stare on his back all the way up the stairs. Jonah didn't care. But by the time he made it to his room, he only had enough energy left to fall down on a chair and stare at the wall. The reality of what he'd heard sank in, causing him to go still as he sat there in the growing dusk.

His mother had fallen for a married man. And she'd accused that man of raping her. And Jonah was the product of that act.

He'd found out the truth at last. But not on his own and not from Alice. She'd gone behind his back to solve the mystery of his past, and yet she'd somehow managed to keep that from him. Just the way everyone else had managed to keep it from him. How could he have trusted her?

He could never forgive her for this. He could never forgive any of them for this. And he'd never forgive Alice for making him fall in love with her.

Finally, stiff from sitting so long, he got up and gathered his things. Then he called Burt Holland and told the construction foreman he was now in charge. "I have to go back to Shreveport but I'll call and check in. I'm counting on you to get things done, Burt."

"When will you be back?" Burt asked.

"I don't know," Jonah said before hanging up.

But he did know. He did know. That sweet illusion of home had been shattered, right along with that first grasp of hope he'd felt when he'd held Alice in his arms. And because of that, he couldn't come back here.

Instead, he'd find his mother and ask her why everyone had lied to him for so very long.

* * *

Alice sat with her head in her hands, a great fatigue pulling at her body. The maternity waiting room was quiet now. Most of the visitors had gone home to bed and only a few anxious husbands and proud grandmothers hovered around.

Jay was in with Lorene and their new baby boy. Jayson Michael Hobert, weighing in at seven pounds and twelve ounces. He was healthy and hungry even though he'd come a couple of weeks early, and Lorene was tired but full of joy. She'd made it through the pregnancy after giving all of them a big scare.

"How's she doing?"

Alice looked up to find Samuel Guidry standing over her. The old man looked as tired as she felt. Surprised that he'd come to the hospital so late, she nodded. "She's fine." Alice gave him all the vital statistics on the baby. "Thank you for…coming to check."

"May I sit?"

Alice motioned to a chair.

He unfolded onto the cushioned seat, his bones creaking and his breath sharp with the effort. "I did a lot of thinking tonight. Your sister…seeing the ambulance take her away like that…brought it all back, all the pain and the lies and the secrecy. I had to watch them take my wife away in an ambulance and she never came home. She died in the hospital. I wished time and again I'd told her the truth about her son and his shortcomings. I tried to protect her 'cause I loved her. Anyway, tonight I got to wondering how… how Esther fared when she had Jonah."

Alice wanted to lash out at him. How dare he come here now and ask that question after all this time? But she was too tired and too upset to muster up the strength to scream at a broken old man. "Nobody knows what became of her…how she managed after she had Jonah," she said. "All we know is that she left Jonah at an orphanage upstate when he was around four or so. He had a picture of Rosette House with him. We're pretty sure Esther drew that picture when she was young."

"She liked to draw," Samuel said. "I do remember that. She dreamed of going away to some fancy art school. Least that's what Sonny used to tell me."

Alice sat up. "Do you remember where?"

"New York, maybe," Samuel said. "Sonny used to tease her about that. He told her to forget it—she'd never make it to New York. Maybe she did, though."

"Did Sonny talk about her a lot?"

"Only to me," Samuel admitted. "His mama didn't know none of it. It would have killed her. She had such high hopes for that boy." He coughed, then shook his head. "My wife introduced him to the woman he married. She was from a good family and she managed to calm him down some. But… he came over here to Bayou Rosette to do some handy work, trying to earn extra money, and that's when he met Esther. I think it was love at first sight. I only found out about it when things started getting nasty between them. He actually came to me for advice. That was a first."

"And then he came to you again for help."

"He did. And I believed him, only because I knew he loved her and would never intentionally hurt her. So when Esther showed up, starting trouble, I knew what I had to do. I had to protect his mother and him."

"Why didn't you at least listen to Esther and follow through? Wasn't that your job?"

"Should have been. I guess I just didn't want to believe her. Her old man found out and…I think he beat her. After her pa and those mean brothers threatened to blackmail me, I came up with a solution."

"You bought their land and forced them to leave."

"It was a mutual agreement," he said, his tone defensive. "They knew a good thing when they saw it and they were just greedy enough to take the offer. They didn't care about the girl. Just the money." He shifted on the chair then stared down the long hallway. "Now I'm wondering if I did the right thing."

Alice got up to glare down at him. "No, you didn't do the right thing. The right thing would have been to investigate this and get to the truth, good or bad."

He gave her a watery-eyed look. "We could do that now, you and me."

Alice couldn't believe what she was hearing. "You're not serious?"

"You started this, girl," he said, drawing back.

"Yes, and now I'm finished with it," she said. "We broke Jonah's heart back there, or did you fail to notice that?"

"I saw," he said. "And that's why I'm here now. I...I need to make it up to the boy."

"Too little, too late," Alice said. "If you really want to make it up to him, and if you have any pull left around here, you'll find Esther Mayeaux and let her see her son. You owe her and Jonah that, at least."

"What if she doesn't want to see him?"

Alice's mind raced as she sank back down in her chair. She'd never considered that. Never once. Even when Dotty had tried to warn her that sometimes knowing the truth wasn't the best thing.

"I can't answer that," she said. "I know I've hurt Jonah and I don't know if he'll ever forgive me. Even if I did agree to find his mother, it would only make him hate me even more. He wanted me to stay out of it, but I didn't."

Samuel got up, bent and worn. "Well, he already hates me so I got nothing to lose." With that, he tipped his hand at her then said, "Tell the new mama I'm glad things turned out good for her and the little one."

"I will," Alice replied.

Then she watched as he slowly made his way to the elevator. And left her sitting alone in the quiet of the hospital waiting room, wondering where Jonah was right now.

Chapter Seventeen

Three days later, Jonah sat in his high-rise office in Shreveport, staring out the wide window at the Red River swirling down below. He watched as a piece of driftwood floated by, caught up in the current.

He felt about as helpless as that piece of water-soaked wood. Still numb from what he'd heard that night on the bayou, he wondered for the thousandth time why Alice hadn't just immediately told him what she'd discovered. If she'd only been honest with him…

You would have still been angry, he told himself.

Yes, he would have been angry but not at her. Maybe mad at her for being so stubborn, but he could have handled that. His anger though, would have been the same.

Because he knew more now than he'd ever wanted to know about his mother, yet he still didn't know the whole story. And tracking her down wasn't easy. He'd gone through death certificates on Web sites in every Louisiana parish and so far he hadn't found one bearing her name. He didn't know if she'd even stayed in the state. And he'd tried tracking down the two brothers. One was dead and the other one was out of the country, working for an oil company. Their father, his other grandfather, had died fifteen years ago.

He was seriously considering hiring a private investigator. He had to do something, anything, to end this constant wondering and imagining. For now, he tried busying himself with daily updates from Burt, including pictures and e-mails and countless phone calls. His community was coming to life without him there to watch it. Bayou Branch would soon be a reality. But the reality of his life had taken a twisted turn.

He was alone again. All alone and in love with a woman who'd done the same thing his family had. She'd kept the truth from him. How could he forget something like that?

In spite of his anger, he wondered what

Alice was doing right now. Had she noticed that the frame of the model house was now up, that the walls were beginning to take shape? Had she missed him at all? Had he been too hasty to just walk away like that?

A knock on the door brought him out of his thoughts. "Yes?"

His secretary came in, smiling softly. "Jonah, there's a man here to see you. He doesn't have an appointment, but he says it's urgent."

"Who is it?"

"A Mr. Samuel Guidry."

Jonah's shock must have registered on his face.

"Should I tell him to wait?" she asked, uncertainty in her words.

"No, I can't see him—"

But the door to his office slammed open and Samuel Guidry filled it. "You need to see me, Jonah. It's very important. I think I know where your mother is."

Jonah looked past his surprised secretary to the man hunched like a grizzly bear inside the door. Waving a hand to reassure the frightened woman, he said to Samuel, "Come in. I'll give you five minutes."

"I won't take that long," Samuel said,

stepping aside to let the secretary pass. As she closed the door, he looked around the office. "You did pretty good for yourself."

"No thanks to my parents."

"No, no thanks to them. They didn't do right by you, that's for sure."

"So you're here to make up for that?"

Samuel slowly worked his way into the high-back chair across from Jonah's desk. "I guess I am." He gave Jonah a plaintive stare. "I don't have much time left on this earth so I'd like to be able to make amends."

"To ease your guilt?"

"Maybe. But…mainly to set things right. I was a hard, mean law officer, but I never used my position to break the law. And this thing with your parents—that was the only time I ever bent any rules. I've regretted it since, I can tell you."

He tapped a wrinkled finger on the desk. "After I bought the Mayeaux place, it sat dormant for years. I kept waiting for the right buyer to come along. And I think he did, son. I placed the ad to sell it right after the doctor told me my heart was shot. If ever there was a sure sign from the good Lord to make things right, I'd say this is it. You're doing a good thing with that old place. You're gonna wipe away all the bad memories and build new ones. Your parents would be proud of that and…I'm proud for you, too. It kinda makes sense, things coming full circle. And I guess that's why I'm here now. To bring things full circle so you can get on with your life."

"But justice hasn't come full circle, has it?" Jonah pushed away from his desk, then sat back in his chair. "Did you ever wonder if maybe my mother was telling the truth?"

"Many times," Samuel said, nodding. "But…it just didn't add up. She loved your father and he loved her, even if that love was doomed. I just had a gut instinct that something didn't make sense. But I never investigated it."

"And what is your gut telling you now?" Jonah asked, his bitterness toward this man brooking no pity.

"That I was right all along," Samuel answered, his tone firm. "I called in a lot of favors to get it done, but I found your mama, son. She's living in Taos, New Mexico. And…after a long conversation, she's willing to see you. She wants to set the record straight once and for all. But a warning—you might not like what she has to say."

He threw a folder across the desk. "Here's all the information. I hope it helps." He got up, using the desk as leverage. "Oh, and any time you want to get to know me a little better, you can find me right there in Century, Louisiana. Just don't wait too long, you hear?"

Jonah watched, unable to say anything, as Samuel turned to leave. What was there to say to this man, anyway? Samuel had been the last link he'd needed to find his past, and now he wasn't so sure he wanted to see that past. The picture he'd always had in his mind couldn't match the ugliness of what he was slowly piecing together.

Samuel turned at the door. "And you might consider cutting Alice some slack. She wasn't searching for a story to put in print. She was trying to help you, but she dreaded telling you all of this and that's why she held back. She was trying to put off breaking your heart. I think she wanted to protect you, same as I wanted to protect the ones I loved all those years ago. Just consider that before you write her off, son."

Thanksgiving morning rose over the bayou in a crisp, shining golden halo that made the woods and water shimmer right into the noon hour, the fall sunshine dappling the turning leaves with a paintbrush-soft clarity. A lone egret strolled gracefully through the shallow water just beyond the old bridge, ignoring the orange-and-yellow tallow tree leaves falling all around. Two squirrels chased each other and quarreled inside the big live oak across the way.

The park was almost completely finished. Stone benches sat in place around the crushed shell pathways, and azaleas and crape myrtles formed a meandering path toward the new houses springing up around the curve. The whole place would come alive with pink-and-white blossoms next spring. But first, it had to get through winter.

Alice shifted her gaze to the model house. The frame was up now. But today, the workers were gone and the bayou was quiet. Too quiet. She'd grown used to the noise of hammers and drills and construction crews laughing and talking.

And she missed the noise of Jonah's truck coming up the rut-filled dirt lane. She missed the sound of his voice, calling to her across the water. She missed seeing him waiting just outside her door—waiting to be invited in. She missed Jonah so much, the ache stayed centered inside her stomach like an open wound. Would he ever come back here?

"Hey, I think your dressing-stuffing stuff is burning," Jay said from behind her. "Want me to take it out of the oven?"

Alice turned, her smile forced. "I'll get it. I'm not sure how eatable it's going to be, but at least we have food."

"Well, it smells just the same as always—shrimp, crawfish and corn bread with lots of chicken broth mixed in. Can't go wrong with that combination."

"We did follow Lorene's recipe to the letter," Alice said, thinking Jay always managed to roll with the punches. "I appreciate your help, by the way."

"My fried turkey is just about perfect," he countered, the look of hope in his eyes making her smile. "We might get more kitchen duty around here if we do a good job today."

Jay had tried so very hard to keep her cheered up this morning, but she wasn't so sure she could muster much past a fake smile. Lorene was doing her part, too, always making sure Alice got to help with little Jayson's care and well-being. Her sister's way of reminding her that even in the midst of grief and pain, life was still precious.

Alice went to the oven and pulled out the dressing. "You're right. It does smell like dressing, at least," she said, putting it on the counter to cool. "And I have string beans and sweet potatoes, bread from the Bayou Inn and two pies—pumpkin and pecan, thanks to Paulette."

"You did okay for a first effort," Lorene said as she came into the kitchen. "Thanks for helping out today."

"Not a problem. How did you and Jayson sleep last night?"

"He was hungry," Lorene said with a grin. "So…I didn't get a good night's sleep, but that's okay. We'll both have a long nap after dinner. Then we'll go over to visit with Jay's folks for a late supper, if we're still hungry, which I doubt." She glanced around. "Where's our guest?"

"Dotty should be here soon," Alice said, glad for Dotty's no-nonsense attitude. It had kept her sane these last few days and she could use a good dose of it today. "She's bringing some dip and vegetables."

"That sounds good," Lorene said. "I'm hungry now that I've gotten Jayson settled."

Alice put the rest of the food on the counter. "We'll leave it all here to stay warm, then transfer it to the table after Dotty gets here. I think that's it."

"Why don't you sit down and rest a bit?" Lorene asked. "We haven't had a chance to talk much lately."

Alice understood what Lorene was asking. She was worried about her baby sister. Lorene had always worried about Alice. After Jay had brought her and little Jayson home, Alice had told Lorene the whole story about Jonah's past. What did it matter now who she told? Wishing she could take away that concern in her sister's eyes, she nodded. "I could use a rest."

They went into the den while Jay went out back to check on his prized Cajun fried turkey that was cooking in a big vat of oil in a turkey fryer, the spicy scent wafting through the yard.

"Are you really okay?" Lorene asked, her own fatigue showing in the dark circles underneath her eyes.

"I'm fine. I've tried to stay busy." Alice glanced out the window. "I keep expecting to see Jonah out there, waiting. I wish I'd been honest with him."

"He's hurting from things you had no control over, honey. You can't blame yourself for the choices his parents made."

"But...I knew and I didn't warn him. I'll never forget the look he gave me when Samuel Guidry blurted out the truth."

Lorene touched a hand to Alice's arm. "It's Thanksgiving—and God is watching and waiting, too. Anything is possible as long as we cling to that."

Alice nodded, but she wasn't so sure. She believed God was all-knowing and all-forgiving, but she just couldn't put as much hope in humanity. Jonah was hurt and angry and confused. How could God make that right?

Then she heard the door opening and Dotty walked in. "Why so glum?" she asked in her pragmatic way. "I figured you'd at least smile since I actually showed up."

Alice did smile. "I'm so glad you're here."

"Then let's get this show on the road," Dotty said. "I'm sure ready for a feast." She winked at Alice. "And, I have to get home and wait for a phone call."

"What kind of phone call?" Alice asked, curious about the spark of life in Dotty's eyes.

"From my ex-husband," Dotty said,

shaking her head. "Okay, after what happened with you and Jonah…I called him…just to talk." She put her hands in the pocket of her long peasant skirt. "He was actually glad to hear from me and he thinks we made a big mistake—getting a divorce."

"I think you did, too," Alice said. "But how do you feel about that?"

Dotty shrugged. "I'm not so sure. But all this business with Jonah and you, well, it's taught me to look at things in a different light. I might learn how to forgive myself, after all. We'll see if the man really has made a change of heart."

Alice hugged Dotty close, not caring if her friend wasn't into being hugged. "Dotty, that's so wonderful. I hope things work out this time."

Dotty whispered in her ear. "You'd better—making me confess all of this. If I go back to the Big Easy, you get to be the boss at the *Bayou Buzz*."

Before Alice could react to that news, Jay walked in, carrying a huge turkey on a white platter. "He's all cooled down and ready to carve. I think this is my best bird yet, if I do say so myself."

Alice looked around and saw the blessing

of her life and, in spite of her aching heart, she knew God was with her today. And He'd get her through this. She was going to be okay.

Jonah parked his truck up on the road and walked the short distance to the park. He didn't want anyone to see him wandering around out here. It was close to dusk and the chill of the gloaming made the swamp and woods seems quiet and sleepy. This was a time when everyone came in to dinner and families held hands and said grace underneath the glowing light of a dinner table. He still wondered what that was like. He'd always dreaded early evening because it meant he'd go home alone.

He'd had no choice but to come back. He had to end this thing, once and for all. The truth of his past wasn't anything like the pretty picture he'd carried with him all of his life. But the reality was that he'd made a commitment to the people of this town, and he aimed to finish that job. The rest he'd have to put in God's hands. Because he was so weary of trying to shoulder the burden on his own.

When he looked up and saw Alice standing on the porch of Rosette House, he remembered the first day he'd seen her there. Maybe Samuel was right; maybe things had come full circle.

Jonah didn't move toward her but instead just stood underneath the old oak, watching as she walked across the yard. She was wearing a striped turtleneck sweater with a flowing brown skirt over her favorite cowboy boots. Her hair was in that careless upswept do, a sliver of a bronzed clip holding the erratic curls at bay.

And she was carrying something. A plate with a piece of pie on it. And one lone candle burning on top.

When she came to the top of the curving bridge, she stopped to look across at him. And Jonah figured she was waiting for him to meet her halfway.

He walked toward her, his eyes on her. When he got a foot away, he said, "Hi."

"Hi," she said back, her hands holding the plate of pie close. "I remembered it's your birthday. All week long." When he didn't say anything, she balanced the plate on the wide bridge railing, then turned to ask, "So…how are you?"

"Not so good," he admitted. "I've been away."

"We noticed."

"No, I mean, I…found my mother. Samuel tracked her down."

He saw the sharp intake of Alice's breath. "That's good, isn't it?"

"Not so good, actually." He looked across at her, his fingers brushing the aged, splintered wood of the railing. "It seems she took me to that orphanage because…well, because she wanted to be free and clear. She wanted me to have a good life and she didn't think she could give me one. She tried, for years, but…every time she looked at me she remembered all that had happened. All that she'd done. And so, her guilt caused her to run. She abandoned me and she never looked back. Never once."

Alice didn't move, but he saw the sheen of shock clouding her eyes. "What about justice? Didn't she ever want justice, at least?"

"There is no justice," he said, his tone flat. "There was no rape, Alice. She panicked and made that up to try and force the issue. When it backfired, her father and brothers got greedy and tried to blackmail the sheriff and my…dad, just like Samuel told us. They took the money and they left and then…I came along. By then, Esther had taken up with another man and he didn't really like having a kid around. So she left me and she headed to New Mexico. And that's that."

Alice stepped toward him, but he couldn't move. "But…she had to be glad to see you? Jonah?"

He shook his head. "She's not glad. She doesn't want anything to do with me. She thinks it's better that I just forget all about her." He glanced over at Rosette House, his gaze taking in the shadows of light and darkness as the sunset began to fade behind him. The house, with Alice's silhouette just in front of it, was washed in a golden-pink brush of dusk. It had never looked more beautiful. Alice had never looked more beautiful. "She's a painter. Her paintings are lovely." He shrugged. "She left that sketch with me because she wanted me to have that kind of life one day, the life she never had. She told me she sat over here day in and day out, dreaming of being on the other side of this water. But that never happened. She wants that for me, if nothing else."

Alice reached out a hand to him. "Jonah, I'm here. I'm here. Do you understand? I'm so sorry for everything, but I'm here and we can start over. You and me. And I promise you, you can have that pretty picture. We can make it happen."

He almost backed away. Almost. But the weariness was taking over again. And he thought about all the years he'd been so alone, holding himself back, watching—just watching. "I guess I've had this image in my mind for so long, I just thought it would all be perfect. You know, if I could just find her, talk to her, understand her. And now that I do—I can't seem to feel anything. Nothing is ever simple, is it? And nothing is ever really perfect, not the way we have it in our mind."

"No," Alice said, her hand still reaching. "No, but…we have to try. We have to do the best we can, and when we mess up we turn to God and each other for comfort. Jonah, let me help you, please? Let me…love you."

He looked over at her, that huge swelling of pure love filling his heart again. "I blamed you," he said, his voice cracking. "I blamed you, but you were just the messenger. And I've blamed God, too, but He didn't cause any of this. Greed and revenge and anger and manipulation—that's what caused this. That and a young girl stuck in poverty and pain." He put a hand up, then let it drop. "I just need it to be over, Alice. I just need it to be over."

"It is," she said, tears streaming down her face. "It is. We can start fresh. I can't promise it'll be perfect, but I can tell you this—if you take my hand and let me help you, I'll work so hard…to show you what a real family is like, I promise. Jonah, please?"

He saw her hand, saw how she was shaking as she moved toward him and without another thought, he reached out to her, taking her hand in his so he could draw her close there in the middle of the bridge. "Alice," he said, whispering her name as he held her tight and took in the scent of jasmine in her curls. "Alice." He kissed her face, tasted her tears and then kissed her on the lips. "Alice."

"I love you, Jonah. I love you."

He savored those words, letting them slip over him like a warm wash of water. "I love you, too." Then he looked up and into her eyes. "You might have to show me. I haven't had much practice, but I love you."

"I'll be glad to show you," she said, sniffing. "Make a wish and blow out your candle before the wind does it for you."

He lifted his head and closed his eyes, taking a quick breath and inhaling toward the plate. The candle flickered out.

"What did you wish for?"

"This," he said, wrapping his arms around her. "Always this." Then he buried his nose against her hair. "You smell like pumpkin pie."

"I have both pecan *and* pumpkin pie," she whispered. "I'm willing to share."

"Did you cook it?"

"No. Paulette made it."

He groaned. "I haven't had a decent meal since I left this place. I'm starving."

"Then I'll feed you," she said. "You'll never be hungry again, even if I can't cook."

Jonah smiled for the first time in days. "Are we crazy, Alice? Can we really make this work?"

She stepped back, then swept her hand toward the frame of the house behind him. "Look. See what you've done, Jonah? You built on solid ground. You created something good out of something bad. Yes, we can do this."

"I'm calling it Bryson Branch," he told her. "That hasn't changed. But I think I'll call the park something else. Maybe Alice Park."

Tears formed in her eyes again.

"Are you sure? Maybe you should name it after Esther. And maybe you shouldn't give up on her yet, either."

He glanced back at the land across the bridge. "You might be right. It can serve as a reminder to me every day to be a better person—for you."

"You are the *better* person," Alice said, pride in her words.

"And Miss Betty Nell—I haven't forgotten her house. We start on it next week. I've secured a low-cost loan so she can afford it."

"She'll be so happy."

"What if I can't make *you* happy?" he asked, his doubts moving like shadows across his mind.

"You will," Alice said as she tugged him across the bridge, and toward Rosette House. "I believe in you, Jonah. That's all you need to know."

Jonah stopped her at the foot of the bridge, kissing her again. "Let me get that piece of pie." He grabbed it and then smiled as she took him by the hand.

"C'mon inside," she said, her smile bright with joy, her eyes sparkling with hope. "And, Jonah?"

"What?"

"Welcome home."

Jonah looked up at the house he'd dreamed about for so long. And he realized the picture had finally changed. Now he had his own house across the way and the hope of sharing his life there with the woman he loved.

Then he heard the sweet cry of a baby coming from inside Rosette House and he closed his eyes and thanked God for showing him the real meaning of a home.

It truly was a gift of wonder.

* * * * *

Dear Reader,

Thanksgiving is always a time to come home to family. But in this story, Jonah Sheridan had never had the strength of a real home and family in his life. When he saw how close Alice and her sister, Lorene, were, he envied them. And he longed for a family of his own. Alice had taken her blessings for granted. She had to show Jonah that he could have the kind of life she'd always known. But Alice hadn't really given herself over to God, so she was also missing the strength that faith can bring. Together, they learned that with God anything is possible. Including finding the gift of wonder in the simple, everyday treasures of life.

Since Louisiana has been changed forever by hurricanes, I wanted to write a story that showed the hope of rebuilding—both our physical homes and our home in God's love. I hope you will consider taking some time to say a prayer for all the people in Louisiana and all along the Gulf Coast who have suffered through the loss of their homes. May they'll all find their way back one day.

Until next time, may the angels watch over you. Always.

Lenora Worth

QUESTIONS FOR DISCUSSION

1. Why did Jonah come to Bayou Rosette? What was he really hoping to do once he got there?

2. Why was Alice so wary of Jonah? Have you ever lost trust in someone?

3. Did Alice resent her sister's happiness? Has this ever happened to you?

4. Do you think Lorene resented Alice because Lorene had to sacrifice things in order to take care of her younger sister?

5. Why do you think it was so important for Jonah to find out the truth about his mother?

6. Do you think Alice should have minded her own business, or was she right to be curious about Jonah's past?

7. Do you think Alice should have been honest with Jonah about doing research on his behalf?

8. Do you think Jonah was doing the right thing in trying to rebuild the bayou houses?

9. Do you think it's important as a Christian to help the environment and to try and conserve our planet's natural beauty?

10. Have you ever gone into a devastated community to help rebuild after a natural disaster? Why do you think this kind of mission work is so important?

11. Why did Jonah always stand just outside of Rosette House? Have you ever been afraid to become a part of someone's life?

12. Do you think Jonah will eventually forgive his mother? Do you understand her motives for abandoning him?

Adam hoisted himself onto the balcony, swinging one leg at a time over the rail. He hoped he hadn't been spotted by a compound guard.

But the sight of Emma Pickering peering out from behind the curtain put his concerns to rest. He had done the right thing.

"Good morning, Miss Pickering." He leaned against the white window frame.

"Mr. King." She was almost breathless. "I cannot speak with you."

"But I need to talk. Mind if I come inside?"

"Indeed, sir, you may not take another step! Are you mad?"

He couldn't hold back a grin. "No more than most. I figure anyone who would leave home and travel all the way to Africa has to be a little off-kilter."

"You refer to me, I suppose? I'll have you know I'm here for a very good reason."

"Railway inspection, is it? Or nursing?"

Emma looked even better than he had thought she might—and he had thought about her a lot.

"Speaking of nursing," he ventured.

"Mr. King, I have already told you I'm unavailable. Now please let yourself down by that…that rope thing, and—"

"My lasso?"

"You must go down again, sir. This is unseemly."

Emma was edgy this morning. Almost frightened. Different from the bold young woman he had met yesterday.

He couldn't let that concern him. Last night after he left the consulate, he had made up his mind to keep things strictly business with Emma Pickering.

"I'll leave after I've had my say," he told her. "This is important."

"Speak quickly, sir. My father must not find you here."

"With all due respect, Emma, do you think I'm concerned about what your father thinks?"

"You may not care, but I do. What do you want from me?"

"I need a nurse."

"A nurse? Are you ill?"

"Not for me. I have a friend—at my ranch."

Her eyes deepened in concern as she let the curtain drop a little. "What sort of illness does your friend have? Can you describe it?"

Adam looked away. How could he explain the situation without scaring her off?

"It's not an illness. It's more like…"

Searching for the right words, he turned back to Emma. But at the first full sight of her face, he reached through the open window and pulled the curtain out of her hands.

"Emma, what happened to you?" He caught her arm and drew her toward him. "Who did this?"

She raised her hand in a vain effort to cover her cheek and eye. "It's nothing," she protested, trying to back away. "Please, Mr. King, you must not…"

Even as she tried to speak, he stepped through the balcony door and gathered her into his arms. Brushing back the hair from her cheek, he noted the swelling and the darkening stain around it.

"Emma," he growled. "Who did this to you?"

She fell motionless, silent in his embrace. No wonder she had shied like a scared colt. She hadn't wanted him to know.

Torn with dismay that anyone would ever harm this beautiful woman, he felt an irresistible urge to kiss her.

"Emma, you have to tell me…." Realization flooded through him. A pompous, nattily dressed English railroad tycoon had struck his own daughter.

"Leave me, I beg you. You have no place here."

"Emma, wait. Listen to me." Adam caught her wrists and pulled her back toward him. He'd never been a man to think things through too carefully. He did what felt right.

"I want you to come with me," he told her. "I need your help. Let's go right now. Emma, I'll take care of you."

"I don't need anyone to take care of me," she shot back. "God is watching over me."

"Emma!" Both turned toward the open door where Emma's sister stood, eyes wide.

"Emma, go with him!" Cissy crossed the room toward them. "Run away with him, Emma. It's your chance to escape—to become a nurse, as you've always wanted.

You'll be safe at last, and you can have your dream."

Emma turned back to Adam.

"Come on," he urged her. "Let's get moving."

* * * * *

Will Emma run away with Adam and finally realize her dreams of becoming a nurse? Find out in THE MAVERICK'S BRIDE, available in September 2009, only from Love Inspired® Historical.